Suddenly, pa
want Lucas t

She very much wanted him to stay. Yet even as she thought this he said he ought to be going.

She swallowed and smiled, but neither of them moved or looked anywhere but deeply at one another. The room stilled, filled with expectant quietness. The space between them became enlivened, electrically charged. Neither was aware of the outside world till the sharp sound of the doorbell split the silence in two.

Janet Ferguson was born at Newmarket, Suffolk, and during her going-out-to-work days was a medical secretary, working in hospitals both in London and the provinces. It was when she moved to Saltdean in Sussex that she settled down to writing general fiction novels, then moved on to medical romance. She says, 'As to where I get my ideas for plots (writers are always asked that), they come when I'm walking my dog on the Downs; the wind whispers them into my ear...do this...do that...say this...say that...go home and write it *now*. With the elements to inspire me, not to mention two nurses in my family, I aim to keep writing medical romance, and to "plot till I drop".'

Recent titles by the same author:

THE MIDWIFE BRIDE
FALLING FOR A STRANGER
THE LOCUM AT LARCHWOOD
A SURGEON TO TRUST

A SURGEON
FOR KATE

BY
JANET FERGUSON

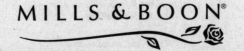

All the characters in this book have no existence outside the imagination of the author, and have no relation whatsoever to anyone bearing the same name or names. They are not even distantly inspired by any individual known or unknown to the author, and all the incidents are pure invention.

*First published in Great Britain 2004
Harlequin Mills & Boon Limited,
Eton House, 18-24 Paradise Road, Richmond, Surrey TW9 1SR*

© Janet Ferguson 2004

ISBN 0 263 83881 1

*Set in Times Roman 10½ on 12 pt.
03-0204-50589*

*Printed and bound in Spain
by Litografia Rosés, S.A., Barcelona*

CHAPTER ONE

IT WAS on Kate's second day as an agency nurse at Seftonbridge General Hospital that the surgical registrar was pointed out to her by one of the regular nurses.

The two young women were in Sister's office, checking the drugs cupboard, and as the task needed concentration Kate could have done without Jean's nagging and prompting to look through the viewing window into the ward.

The October sun, low in the sky, for it was nearly teatime, lay in yellow bands over the first half-dozen beds, and it was there at bed number three that the much drooled-over Lucas Brown was standing with Sister Rooke.

'You've go to agree,' Jean persisted, 'that he's a blood-tingling sight.'

'Not bad, what I can see of him.' Kate risked another look. Actually, *all* she could see was the back of his head with its cap of thick dark hair, the nape of his neck, his white surgical coat and a length of beige-trousered leg. Then, as he swivelled slightly to chat with a patient, she saw his face in profile and, yes, it looked good. Her interest sparked. She liked the cut of his jaw—square and taut—and his nose was of the powerful sort. She judged his height to be six feet or a little less, perfectly suiting his build.

'He catches the eye, he's striking,' she said guardedly, returning to her pills.

'He doesn't suit his name, though.' Jean chattered on. 'I mean, in no way does he look like a Mr Brown!'

'Oh, I don't know.' Furtively Kate slewed her eyes windowwards. He had moved, she saw, and was passing down the ward with a swing to his stride, which was in no sense a swagger, more an ease of movement as though this was a man who was comfortable with himself. 'There have been several very notable Mr Browns throughout the course of history,' she added, 'and when you put his first name, Lucas, in front of it, I think it suits him perfectly. Has he been here long?' she queried offhandedly, trying to mask her interest.

'About a year,' Jean supplied. 'He came from York. He's just been up there on holiday, seeing friends, I suppose, and before you ask, he's not married, but he's seeing someone—Claire Jevons, our orthopaedic sister. She lives in the same block of flats as him, which must make for convenience.'

Kate was about to say something flip when a loud thump came on the door, and one of the auxiliary staff entered, holding a bunch of bronze chrysanthemums.

'For Mrs Simmons,' she said. 'Would you like me to take them in?'

'No, thanks, Zelda, leave them with me.' Jean held out her hands for the flowers.

'OK, suit yourself.' Zelda banged her way out. She was renowned for her noisiness and bouncy ways, but the patients loved her, she cheered them up. Kate wondered why she'd been stopped from taking the flowers in.

'You take them.' Jean passed them over. 'Then you can get a good look at Lucas. Ava Simmons is the lady with a hernia in bed nineteen.'

'Yes, I know. I was here yesterday, remember, I

prepped her for surgery,' Kate said agreeably enough, but making her point just the same. Flowers in hand, she entered the ward, taking a wide sweep past Lucas and the nursing sister, her eyes fixed on bed nineteen.

Ava Simmons's main discomfort was down her right thigh, where strips of skin had been pared off to darn the space in her abdominal wall after removal of the peritoneal sac. She was sitting by the side of her bed looking tense and unhappy, but her creased face brightened when she saw the flowers.

'They're from Bob, from our greenhouse,' Ava said, all but caressing the blooms. 'He can't visit this afternoon, he's on duty. He's a community nurse, you know.'

'As well as a gardener?' Kate smiled at her.

'Yes, he spends all his spare time growing things, says it balances things out. We've got loads of outside chrysanths coming on, but these are special ones, and all for me... That's my Bob for you...always aims to please.' Her eyes filled with the tears of weakness that so often followed surgery.

'Shall I put them in water for you?' Kate reached for the flowers.

'Please, dear, if you've time.' Ava winced as her leg began to hurt again. 'Mr Brown told me I'd have this sore patch on my thigh, but I didn't realise *how* sore. It's worse than the wound itself. Why couldn't he have stitched me up with the ordinary nylon stuff?'

'Because your own skin makes a far better job of mending the gap. It's well worth a little more suffering to get a good end result,' Kate explained, backing away from the bed straight into the path of Lucas Brown who was less than six paces away. She hadn't heard him coming. He must move like a panther, she thought as their eyes met and clashed, his showing surprise and startled annoyance.

'Who the devil are you?' he snapped.

'A nurse from the agency.' She remained in front of him, indicating the name-badge on her breast.

'*Another one!*' he exclaimed, just as Sister, who'd been caught up with a patient, hurried to join him. Kate, moving away with the flowers, hurried to the doors, but not quite quickly enough to avoid hearing him say, 'Why do we have to keep employing these agency nurses? Surely it would be better to...' But the rest of his utterance was lost to her as she passed into the corridor.

Arrogant so-and-so...! Her cheeks flamed as, in the safety of the sluice, she reached for a vase just as Jean joined her. She was dying to know what had taken place in the ward.

'Well,' Jean demanded, 'what did you think of him? I saw you having a chat.'

'Hardly a chat, more a confrontation.' Kate stripped the elastic band off the flowers and plunged them into the vase. 'Somehow or other,' she added, 'I don't think the sight of me pleased Mr Brown.'

'I bet it did, he's a man after all!' Jean looked with envy at Kate's slender height, at her pinned-up plait of tawny gold hair. Not so very different a shade from the flowers she was arranging. 'Anyway, what did you think of him?' she asked curiously.

'I would say he's very aware of his position. His looks are dramatic, almost sombre. I prefer a man with a twinkle in his eye.'

'I'm dead sure he can twinkle all right, given the occasion!' Jean grinned, standing back to allow Kate to return to the ward. Both girls had seen Sister and

Lucas go into the office, so the coast was clear this time. 'When you come back,' Jean called, 'you can give me a hand getting the side-ward ready for the ulcer patient coming up from Medical tomorrow.'

'Will do,' Kate replied, readily enough. She was the same grade as Jean, but didn't mind her bossiness. Being 'agency' in a sense demoted her, yet accommodated her as well. Because her role was temporary, it could be borne more easily. The truth was, she was thrilled to be back doing surgical nursing. Despite one or two irritations like frowning and sombre-eyed registrars, she was all set to enjoy her sojourn on Guthrie Ward. Why, the whole set-up, she realised, was as good if not better than that of St Mildred's, London, where she'd nursed for the last four years. Yesterday she had met Andrew Chance, the consultant, when he'd come to do a ward round. Like Lucas, he was immaculately dressed, but unlike Lucas he'd made no disparaging remarks, just nodded and said, 'Ah, splendid,' when Sister had told him who she was. Leaving the ward to collect bedding from the store, Kate found herself wondering how head-in-the-air, supercilious Lucas got on with his boss.

As she and Jean made up the bed in the side-ward and checked its equipment, Kate couldn't help but be aware of the view from its windows—that of Princes Parade and St Saviour's College, with its famous chapel alongside. To be back in the university city where she'd taken her nursing degree was a strange experience, for it took her back to her more carefree years. That time could never be repeated, of course, neither would she want it to be, but a long temporary post here, say to Christmas and just beyond, would suit her just fine. She sighed, caught up in her own thoughts.

'You're bushed, aren't you?' Jean said. 'So am I. We're practically done here now, so let's hurry up and finish. We're well over our time.'

Ten minutes later off they went, parting company in the yard, Jean turning left to the bicycle sheds, Kate to the rear of the loading bay where she had left her car. The main parking lot had been full when she'd come on duty this morning, and one of the maintenance staff had guided her round there.

She could see her white car as she rounded the corner, but it wasn't on its own any more. There was another in front of it—sleek, blue and gleaming, and partly obscured by Lucas Brown who was gesticulating like mad. A mechanic was standing with him, and it wasn't until they turned at her approach that she saw the rest of the car, the whole of it, the fearful damage that had been wrought to the front wing and driver's door. It had been bashed…crushed… A shocked sound escaped her. 'What a mess!' came out in a shout, even as she looked at her own car, which was, thankfully, all right. It did look a little strange, however—not quite as she'd parked it.

'Is this yours?' Lucas Brown was pointing straight at it.

'Yes, it is, but what…' she reached his side '…has happened to yours?'

'There was an accident, Nurse.' Ron Barber from the garage took it upon himself to explain. 'Garstons Pharmaceuticals' lorry backed out from the bay, lost control and plunged straight into the doc's car. I saw the whole thing while having me tea—right shock it gave me. At first I thought he'd got yours as well, from where I was sitting.' He was chewing gum, and the smell of spearmint wafted out into the air. 'Still, he gave me all his details.'

'Their insurers had better pay up promptly.' Lucas sounded as though he was about to explode, and who could possibly blame him? Kate thought with a rush of sympathy, her eyes taking in the rest of the Audi, which looked brand new. 'I've only had it a week.' Lucas's words confirmed her ramblings.

'Will you be able to drive it home?' she asked. 'I suppose if the engine is undamaged and you can open and shut the door, and if you haven't got very far to go…' She broke off, feeling a fool, feeling, too, that he definitely thought she was one. It was a minute before he spoke.

'It seems to have escaped your notice,' he said heavily, 'that we're securely locked together!'

'Locked together… What do you mean?' He had her mystified now. Then, following his pointing, disdainful arm, she saw *exactly* what he meant. Their cars were locked, her front bumper entangled with his rear one, the out-of-control lorry having forced the two vehicles into a clinch. So this was why her car didn't look as she'd left it this morning. 'But surely,' she said, going forward to take a closer look, 'it won't take much to jolt them apart.'

It was a kind of bravado, a kind of showing off that made her put her hands under her bumper, half squatting to the task. But she didn't get far, hadn't even begun to brace herself for the lift, before a hand like a trap closed over her shoulder, jerking her back so sharply and violently that her feet nearly left the ground.

'Hold on. What do you think you're doing?' Lucas's

bellow all but split her eardrums as he spun her round on her heels. 'Do you really want to put your hands out of action for the next six months?'

Kate gasped. 'I just thought…'

'Plainly you didn't!'

'Well, there's no need to be so rude.' Kate dragged her jacket back over her shoulder. She glared at him and he at her, their faces close together. He was the taller, but she at five feet seven and a half, and drawn up to her full height, brought them to combative level. She could see every detail of his face—his thick, formidable brows, slate-grey eyes, lean cheeks, long, high-bridged nose and his mouth below it, grimly set, stretching the line of his jaw. Lucas was taking in Kate's features in the same way. 'So what happens now?' Kate stepped back a pace. 'I'm anxious to get home.'

'I'm fetching a jack, so don't you worry!' Ron was speeding off, returning at the double with a colleague and a jack. The two of them got down to business, sniggering.

After a brief struggle the cars were freed, Kate's bumping to the ground. 'Got 'er off your tail now, sir!' Ron's mate was the cheeky kind. Lucas didn't react, but he tipped the two men. Kate saw a note exchange hands.

'With luck,' he said, 'I should be able to get as far as my usual garage.' Then, assisted by Ron, he got the driver's door open, brushing shards of glass from its seat. Getting in, he fitted the key into the ignition, turned it and, hey, presto, the engine sprang into instant life. 'So far so good.' He smiled through the window space at the three people watching him. 'I'm glad yours is all right.' He was looking at Kate as he fastened his seat belt. And then he was moving slowly and carefully towards the exit gates, giving a little toot on his hooter as he turned into the road.

'Crying shame, that's what it is. He hasn't had it long!' Ron remarked to his mate as the two of them walked away, ten pounds the richer, too, so they could afford to sympathise.

As for Kate, she couldn't get over how different Lucas had looked when he'd smiled—much, much younger. Not that he was old, of course, probably thirty-four or -five, maybe a little less. His smile had been youthful, even boyish, bending the lines on his cheeks. His remark about her car had been generous, too, given the circumstances, so he wasn't mean-spirited. That fact stuck out a mile.

She wondered where his flat was as she started her journey home to Cletford Heath, six miles south of Seftonbridge. She was living with her mother, Paula Maybury, just for the time being. But, then, most things are for the time being now, she thought wistfully. She deplored this, for she longed to be settled, to have her own space again. She wasn't really a temporary kind of person, which was why Lucas's scathing comment to Sister had got under her skin so much. Casting him out of her mind with an effort, she was soon passing through the avenue of beeches that heralded the start of the town.

Her mother was head of the physiotherapy department at the Royal Hospital, Cletford. She, like her daughter, was tall, but was more heavily built and handsome rather than pretty. She and Kate rubbed along well enough, although they couldn't be said to be close. Having said that, Paula had been exactly what

Kate had needed after the trauma in London, which had led to her coming home.

Turning into the driveway of Cruse Cottage that evening, Kate could see her mother up in the orchard, burning hedge clippings, dressed in old tracksuit bottoms and a sweater that reached to her knees. After putting the car in the garage, Kate went to join her, coughing in the smoke. 'Fancy doing that now, Mum. It'll be dark in an hour, and what a terrible stink. I could smell it right up the road.'

'I know, I know!' Paula added another forkful to the blaze. 'Why don't you go and have your shower and leave me to clear up? I picked up a Chinese on the way home—you can heat it up if you like.'

'OK,' Kate said resignedly, turning back to the house, which was two cottages knocked into one. It had a view of the heath from its front windows and a glimpse of the riding stables, belonging to the Vernons, from the back. John and Ann Vernon were friends of her mother's and they often met socially.

Over supper Kate told Paula about the incident on the ward with Lucas, and then about the accident to his car. 'And to add insult to injury our bumpers were locked. He was really angry.'

'Now, that I can understand.' Paula buttered a roll with a lavish hand. 'If anyone bashed up my Golf I'd be livid. Good job yours was all right.'

'Mmm,' Kate said, reflecting that those had been Lucas's words.

She and her mother fell silent then, Paula reading at the table, and it wasn't until they had cleared away and were drinking coffee that she said, looking over her half-glasses at Kate, 'You know, I've just made an interesting connection.'

'What do you mean?' Kate stared at her.

'I think your Lucas Brown must be the son of one of my patients. He's arthritic, comes in three times a week for treatment. His name's Gervase—Gervase Brown—and during our conversation yesterday he told me he had a surgeon son who was working at Seftonbridge General. I'm sure he said his name was Lucas and that he was a consultant.'

'Well, then, it *is* him, without a doubt.' Kate gaped a little and her mother laughed.

'It's a small world, darling!'

'Did he tell you anything else about him?' Kate gave up trying not to sound interested. It was never easy to pull the wool over her mother's eyes, so she may as well learn all she could.

'Actually, he did. Once started he went on and on. He's as proud as Punch of his son. It seems he had a post at the Royal in York until about a year ago when he got the position down here. He lives in Seftonbridge, but comes to see his father whenever he can make it. Oh, yes, and he's got a horse, had it brought down from York just recently. It's at livery at Vernons', so Ann must be looking after it.'

'How amazing!' Kate loved horses.

'Interesting, isn't it?' Paula looked amused. 'When he's here, visiting his father, you'll probably meet him out riding.'

'I hope not!'

'Why?'

'Well…' Kate avoided her mother's eyes. 'Well, no one likes meeting colleagues off duty. It's just not the right sort of ground.'

'By the time you do meet him he may no longer be

a colleague if you've been whisked away by the agency to another nursing post.'

'Even so, I'd sooner not run into him,' Kate said stubbornly. 'He's such a controlling kind of man— makes you lack confidence.'

Paula made no comment on this, but asked her daughter if she was riding next Saturday, and Kate told her she was as she was off duty on both Saturday and Sunday.

'You won't forget that I'm in London all Saturday at the physiotherapy conference?'

Kate told her she hadn't and promised to run her to the station early that day. She would ride in the afternoon, she promised herself, and despite the weekend being three days away she found herself looking forward to being in the saddle again. She was a competent horsewoman, but by no means a natural. Her father had taught her to ride ten years ago when she'd been a schoolgirl of sixteen. She had never owned a horse, just hired one from the Vernons, and even when she'd been nursing in London she'd ridden out when she'd been at home. Tom Maybury, her father, had died of pneumonia following an awful bout of flu, and Kate still missed him. So did her mother, and the gap for both of them was still immense. A man's presence— the right man's presence—reassured like nothing else.

Next day, driving along in the early morning traffic to Seftonbridge, Kate's thoughts returned to Lucas. Would she see him again, and would he have hired a car to get him to the hospital? Apparently he had, for as she turned into the entrance gates she spied him at the wheel of a red Volvo. There was the usual stream of cars all manoeuvring for room, but Kate persevered until she found a space in the main car park. She wasn't going to risk a repeat of yesterday and neither, it seemed, was Lucas, for he was making use of the 'Doctors Only' section. This was some distance away, but as they both got out and stood locking their cars, he glanced back and saw her. After a brief hesitation he gave a small acknowledging salute over the sea of glittering roofs. For a second it looked as though he meant to wait for her, but then he moved off, making for the nearest entrance point via A and E.

Kate didn't know whether she was relieved or disappointed—relieved, she thought as, giving him time to vanish, she slowly entered by the same door and queued at the line of lifts.

Guthrie Ward was on the fourth floor and, sailing up in the lift with the rest of the ongoing shift, she felt her spirits rising as well. It was one of those times when she felt glad to be exactly where she was—in the hospital where as a young student nurse she had tried her fledgling wings.

With the hand-over report done and the nurses dispersed on their various tasks, Sister Chloe Rooke put the side-ward patient under Kate's care. June Tredgold had come up from the medical ward to which she had been admitted two days ago, following severe haematemesis—vomiting of blood—at home. A transfusion had helped, but now it seemed that surgical intervention would be the best course. She looked pale and apprehensive, which wasn't surprising. 'I so hoped it wouldn't come to this,' she said, when Kate was prepping her. The Ryle's tube, for aspiration purposes, was still in position, and would remain there during her time in Theatre. She hated the sight and feel of it taped to her cheek. 'What with that and the blood transfusion going into my arm last night, my husband looked all set to faint. I was glad when he went home.'

'This time next week,' Kate said as she checked June's identity bracelet, 'you'll be free of all tubes and feeling much better…in fact, you'll feel a new woman.'

June managed a strained smile. 'Where will my cut be?' she asked.

'Well, that,' Kate replied, 'depends on the surgeon, and I haven't been here long enough to be au fait with Mr Brown's methods, but I would think upper-midline—from your lower chest to your navel.'

'Quite right,' came a voice from the doorway, then Lucas walked over to the bed. 'I'm Lucas Brown, Mrs Tredgold.' He smiled down at her, nodding briefly to Kate as she moved out of his way. 'I'm the surgeon who will be operating on you, I don't think we've met before.'

'No, I saw another surgeon downstairs.' Her eyes, dark-ringed and anxious, watched him pull out a chair and sit down.

'Yes, that will have been our house officer, Peter Graves. Now, if it isn't a silly question, how are you feeling?' He inclined a little towards her.

'Scared witless.' She responded to his smile. And who wouldn't be? Kate thought, not within range of the smile herself but noticing the change in June.

'You've nothing to be afraid of,' he was telling her. 'What you're having is a very run-of-the-mill operation, and you'll be so much better after it. You'll have a much smaller stomach, but it'll be a healthy one—there'll be no fear of you haemorrhaging again. You'll be able to eat most of your favourite foods, but in smaller quantities.'

'It's a gastrectomy, isn't it, that I'm having?' June

touched the front of her operation gown as though indicating the spot.

'A partial gastrectomy,' Lucas corrected, 'and you'll need to be fed intravenously for two or three days afterwards, till your insides have had time to heal.'

'Tubes for ever!' She pulled a face.

'Not quite for ever.' He laughed. 'Although I know time drags in here.' He got up then and left the room, Kate following. 'I'd like her to have her premedication in half an hour,' he said, 'which means I can start operating around half ten.'

They were walking side by side down the corridor *en route* for the main ward. It was only nine o'clock and Kate wondered who else he wanted to see, and where Sister was, not that she didn't feel equal to the task of escorting senior medical staff, she'd done it often enough. In fact, she was thinking as Lucas pushed the doors open for her, it felt exactly right.

'It's the trauma patient I want to see,' he remarked a little tersely. 'I hear the night staff were bulldozed by Casualty into giving her a surgical bed.'

'She needed one, still does,' Kate replied, leading the way to bed twenty-three.

The patient's name was Sandra Peck, a twenty-year-old student, who'd crashed into a bollard on her bicycle the night before. Casualty had written 'when under the influence of drink' on her notes, but whatever it was she was a sorry sight. Her face, especially her nose, was bruised and hugely swollen, one eye nearly closed.

'Hello, Sandra, I'm Lucas Brown, one of the surgeons here. How are you feeling?' Lucas sat down, his eyes running swiftly over her face, noting but not touching. She told him she was all right. 'And I don't want my parents told, they'll fuss and come rushing down here.'

'Do they live far away?' Lucas's fingers were on her radial pulse.

'Wiltshire,' she said, and Kate noticed that one of her front teeth was chipped. She was frowning heavily, too. All she wanted was to be left to rest.

'It's all right, I'm not going to disturb you, Sandra,' Lucas was quick to reassure her. 'Casualty have told us what happened to you, and the extent of your injuries so far as they can tell. Your nose may be fractured, but we can't do much about it till some of the swelling has gone down and you can be X-rayed. Later today one of the nurses will help this along with alternate hot and cold bathing. You could even do it yourself, if you liked. Nurse Maybury here would be only too happy to show you how.'

'Of course,' Kate was quick to say, astonished that Lucas remembered her name. He even smiled at her, too…well, very nearly…or it might have been the tail end of his bedside pleasantness with Sandra.

At the central ward desk, all brisk again, he instructed her to make sure Sandra didn't try to blow her nose. 'It mustn't be packed either, not even if it bleeds again. Once X-rays confirm that it's broken, which I'm pretty sure it is, she can be transferred to Orthopaedics. She'll be their patient, not ours.'

'Poor girl,' Kate was jolted into saying, but all he did was grunt with a downbent head and scribbled in Sandra's notes.

Sister Rooke appeared then, emerging from her office with the senior nursing officer. Lucas went to join them, leaving Kate free to help two post-operative patients out to the washrooms and back. Soon after that it was time for June's premed, Kate telling her to rest quietly and to try not to get out of bed. 'You'll soon be feeling deliciously woozy, as though all your cares are slipping from you,' she said, replacing the syringe in the tray.

'I'll believe that when it happens,' June said, but even as the words left her lips, Kate could see the drugs combination beginning to take effect, the tenseness fading from her features, her mouth becoming relaxed. When the theatre porters came for her just before ten-thirty, she would hardly notice the journey and would take the anaesthetic easily.

The morning wore on, ambulant patients being helped into the day-room. Beds were tidied, patients due for surgery were prepped in rotation. There were a number of callers—the phlebotomist to take venous blood, the physiotherapist to give breathing exercises to three post-op patients. The medical social worker wanted a word with Sister, so did the hospital chaplain, then immediately after the mid-morning drinks trolley had been whirled in and out by Zelda, Peter Graves arrived to do a short round. In the absence of Jean, who was off duty, Sister asked Kate to escort him.

Peter seemed not at all averse to this, and Kate liked him at once, liked the way he came down to her level and his manner with the patients. He was probably, she judged, about her own age—a fair, rugged young man with freckles on the backs of his hands.

It was mid-afternoon before June Tredgold was returned to the side ward. She had been stabilised downstairs in the recovery room attached to the theatre suite, her blood pressure, pulse rate and breathing now normal. The bed was ready for her and she was transferred to it, an infusion running into her arm, the nasogastric tube still in place, a short corrugated drain in her wound.

Kate knew she would be a heavy nursing case, needing to be aspirated at half-hourly intervals over the next two hours. She was still drowsy, but knew where she was and recognised Kate, asking for a drink of water. 'Very thirsty,' she croaked. As the theatre notes indicated that she could have sips of water, Kate let her have this in droplets from a spouted cup, watched by Student Nurse Karen Johnson, who was on ward placement for the week.

'How long has she got to have that tube in her arm?' she asked, without lowering her voice.

'It's called parenteral feeding,' Kate told her out in the corridor. 'Apart from those little sips of water, oral feeding won't be possible for about three or four days. She's Mr Brown's patient and he will decide when it's safe for her to take food by mouth. And, Karen, try to remember not to ask questions over a patient's bed. However ill they are, they can usually hear. In fact, it's amazing what they pick up and fret over, unknown to us. I know Miss Tredgold looks very ill now, but in three or four days' time she'll be a different woman.'

Karen eyed Kate carefully from under her striped fringe, the word 'bossy' flashing through her head, yet even as it did she knew she was being unfair. She was here to learn, wasn't she? That's what ward placement was about, and if she made a gaffe and was told off for it, that was part of it too. So although she didn't say 'sorry' or 'thanks' or even 'I see', she stopped looking truculent, and at Kate's suggestion, went into the ward to help the gall-bladder patient with Parkinson's disease drink her cup of tea.

Lucas arrived on the ward just before Kate was about

to go off duty, and when the ward still had a straggle of visitors. She saw him come through the doors with Sister when she was bathing Sandra Peck's face for the second time that day. He had probably, she thought, been summoned to Mrs Fenn, the goitre patient, who at three days' post-op was still having discomfort and difficulty in swallowing.

'Soluble aspirin should help,' Kate heard him say as they passed her on the way out. 'She'll benefit from the temperature-lowering effect of the aspirin as well.'

Kate supposed he would look in on June, who had already had a visitor—her husband, an anxious-looking man in late middle age. The fact that June hadn't been able to rouse herself to speak to him, combined with her ashen appearance, had brought him rushing from the side-ward into Sister's office. 'I didn't expect... I had no idea...' he had babbled without restraint. 'I mean, all those tubes and she looks *worse*. Is she going to die?'

Kate, who had been in the office at the time, had felt sorry for him, especially when Sister had told him quite bluntly that he shouldn't have come in so soon, or gone in until he'd seen her first. 'If you remember, Mr Tredgold, I did suggest, when you spoke to me last evening, that you hold back for a day or two.'

'Well, yes, yes... I agree, but I thought...' He had brought out his handkerchief. Kate, praying that he wasn't going to break down, had hastily pulled out a chair.

'Now, this time tomorrow,' Sister had gone on carefully, 'Mrs Tredgold will be looking much better. She'll be feeling better too, and glad to see you. In the meantime, we shall take good care of her. She's doing very well so far.'

'Thank you, yes, I know, and I know I shouldn't have come!' He went off up the corridor, blowing his nose, passing June's door with his head well down, not daring to look in again.

'Fat lot of use he's going to be to her if he keeps going to pieces!' Chloe Rooke, who hid a soft heart under a flint exterior, had returned to her paperwork.

Shortly afterwards when Lucas made his appearance, Kate escorted him into the side-ward. She could see them in there as she emptied her bowls in the sluice. It was five o'clock and she was off duty, but even so she doubled back into the ward to see Sandra. She liked the girl and could understand her misery that her accident had been her own fault. Not that anyone on the staff had blamed her for being drunk. Hospitals weren't judgmental, but Sandra was really suffering, inside and out.

Her facial swelling was less, however. Kate could see an appreciable difference since first thing that morning. 'You'll be even better tomorrow,' she told Sandra, backing away from the bed, and then, as had happened yesterday, she all but collided with Lucas, who was right in her path. Alone now, he was turning into the next bed-space to see a patient who'd undergone keyhole surgery two days ago. 'If I could pass, please,' he said, then, without looking at Kate, he whisked the curtain across between the two beds.

'Well, now, Mrs Carson, we'll be discharging you tomorrow,' she heard him say in cheerful tones, as she finally left the ward.

In the staff cloakroom she pulled a navy sweater over her uniform dress. In another month it would be winter and she'd be needing something heavier, not, she thought, feeling regretful, that she would be nursing here then, for she had only ten more days to go. Sighing a little and easing the strap of her bag over her shoulder, she made her way out to the lifts. There was a queue for each one, so she opted for the stairs, as did several others, Lucas being one of them. She had seen him in the queue, looking fidgety with impatience. He wasn't, she decided, a man to be kept waiting, not even by a lift. She moved swiftly to keep ahead of him, but he caught her up one floor down, and kept with her as they descended further, talking shop in jolting tones in tune with his feet.

'I've just had a word with Sister about Sandra Peck,' he said. 'Her facial swelling has subsided noticeably, so she'll be X-rayed tomorrow, then we can pass her on to Orthopaedics for the reduction of her nasal fracture.'

'You sound as though you'll be glad to get rid of her,' Kate jerked out, and caught Lucas's sidelong glance. He made no comment and she felt abashed, longing to temper her words. It was plain that Sandra shouldn't be taking up a surgical bed, but he'd spoken so blithely about passing her on, as though she were a parcel in the post.

'Don't attempt to wrongfoot me on this, Nurse,' he said as they reached the ground floor. 'You've plainly spent a good deal of time on the girl, and brought about a good result, but tomorrow she'll be transferred, which will not only release a much-needed bed but will leave you free to ply your considerable skills to better advantage.'

After a polite 'Goodnight' and a mouth twitch which could have been the start of a smile, he shouldered his way through the crowd to the doors, leaving Kate standing where she was, mentally gritting her teeth. He had complimented her on her nursing, yet somehow or other had made his praise sound hollow, delivered as it had been with what she could only describe as a derisory glint in his eye. They just didn't see eye to eye, she thought, not that it mattered. It was just one of those things.

The next day it was as he'd forecast. Sandra's X-ray clearly showed fractures of the nasal bones and deviation of the septum and without ado she was transferred to Orthopaedics. By teatime that afternoon her bed had been filled by a woman of fifty in for a hiatus hernia repair.

It was Friday before Kate saw Lucas again, and that was during a teaching round headed by the consultant, Andrew Chance. Full teaching rounds, as she well knew, were practically a state occasion. Seated at the nurses' station, she saw the procession come in—Mr. Chance leading the way, Lucas a step behind, followed by Sister, the six medical students bringing up the rear.

They fanned out and grouped round the first bed—that of Mrs Fenn, the goitre patient now five days post-op. Not everyone was subject to this close scrutiny, for although Andrew Chance in no way apologised for his retinue of students, he made a point of asking each patient if she minded them being there. Most didn't, and this morning—apart from those sleeping—there were no abstainers. The round took ages and Sister was having a hard job to hide her impatience. In her eyes teaching rounds were a necessary evil, but the time they took and the work they held up put the ward routine out of gear.

When this one was finished the lunch trolleys were waiting to be wheeled in. Kate was on supervisory duty and was walking alongside a trolley with the diet sheets in her hand when Lucas passed her, being the last to leave. And perhaps it was because the round had gone off well that he turned back for a second to have a word with her.

'And how are you today?' he asked, watching her stop Karen Johnson, in the nick of time, from giving one of the light-diet patients a plate of chicken and greens.

'Oh, all right, I think.' She could only give him half her attention, but Sister filled in the gap.

'She's more than all right, she's much valued here and we shall be sorry when she goes.'

'Short assignment, is it?' he asked unconcernedly, his attention wandering.

'I've another week to go,' Kate replied, but could have saved her breath, for he was moving away with that air-cushioned stride of his, Sister at his heels.

He was at the wheel of the red Volvo ahead of Kate as she turned onto the Cletford Road that evening bound for home. She soon lost him, though, or he lost her. He drove competently and fast, just like he did everything else, she supposed. He was confident plus. She further supposed—rightly, as it happened—that he was spending the weekend with his father. All she hoped was that she wouldn't meet him at the Stables. But it was unlikely, surely, that their times would co-incide, especially as she was riding tomorrow afternoon. Somehow or other she felt sure that Lucas Brown was an early morning man.

CHAPTER TWO

AS THINGS turned out, Kate was unable to get to the riding stables until late on Saturday. She had no sooner finished a sandwich lunch and gone upstairs to change when the doorbell rang, and there on the step was Natalie Green, an old schoolfriend, with a baby on her hip. She was down from Newcastle, she said, visiting her parents. 'I just had to come and see you, Katy, and show you Ben. Mum said you were living at home now and had left London for good.'

'Well, I don't know about for good, but for the time being, anyway.' Kate blenched a little as the heavy, dribbly Ben was launched into her arms.

'It must be three or more years since we met,' Natalie chattered on, regarding her son from this new viewpoint, leaning forward to wipe his nose.

'It must be about that, I think,' Kate said, leading the way into the sitting room and handing Ben back to his mother. To tell the truth, she was surprised that Natalie had made contact again. They had never been all that friendly, but perhaps it was a case of wanting to show her baby off, which was natural, of course. If only she'd telephoned first, though, not just dropped in. Carefully Kate explained that she was going out, then quickly added, seeing her friend's crestfallen face, that she needn't do so right away.

Even so, it was close on three before Natalie left, driving off in a cream estate car, Ben in his baby seat in the back. Kate could hardly conceal her impatience as she stood there waving them off. It would be very nearly shutting-up time before she got to the stables. Ann Vernon liked her horses back in their boxes and rugged up by half past four. Still, a short ride was better than no ride at all, Kate told herself, striding the quarter-mile from the back of the cottage towards the Vernons' premises, smoothly lithe in jodhpurs and sweater, tawny hair in a ponytail to complement her horse.

Anticipation, amounting to thrill, at the thought of the ride ahead gripped her as she reached the stables and stepped into the yard. Crossing it, and waving to Iris, the stablehand, who would get her mount ready for her, she breathed in the smell of horse and hay, and leather and dung, before going over to the tack-room to collect her hard hat. Standing out in the yard again, buckling it round her chin, she was just about to make her way down to Iris when she heard the slow clop of hooves behind her—someone coming in from their ride. Turning to greet whoever it was, for she knew most of the riders, she was startled to find herself looking at an unknown massive black stallion, whilst on its back, looking practically skyborne, was the imperious Lucas Brown.

Her mouth opened and shut. Her neck cricked. Why is he here *now*? she thought as she stared up at the dark, handsome, brooding face looking down at her. She had been so sure he would ride that morning, which had been naïve of her for as the horse belonged to him and not to the stables, he could come and go as he pleased.

As he dismounted and his face came more level with hers, she managed to acknowledge his 'Hello, Kate Maybury', which had come some seconds ago.

'How surprising to see you!' She managed to smile.

'Surely not,' he said, half-turned from her, grappling with his horse. Then, bunching the reins in one hand, he pivoted to face her. 'It would have been even more surprising if we hadn't met here, sooner or later. My father told me you rode out from the Vernons' and lived nearby, so I thought it was on the cards that your mother might have given you the same information in reverse.'

'Well, yes, she did mention something.' Kate could feel herself getting hot.

'There you are, then, no mystery.' Lucas smiled, his grey eyes surveying her from under the brim of his hat.

He was making her feel foolish again. He's always so right, she thought rebelliously, turning to his horse. 'He's superb, isn't he?' Her voice shook.

'Every black inch of him, yes. He's called Hercules.' Lucas slapped the great creature's neck whilst Hercules, gratified by so much praise, bent his head in a posing attitude, inviting more of such talk.

'He's waiting for you to stroke his nose. He won't bite you, you know!' Lucas said in taunting voice, which Kate rose to at once.

'I'd hardly be here if I was nervous of horses,' she told him with quiet force as she fondled the velvet muzzle. 'Have you had him long?' she asked, breaking the small silence.

'I've *known* him for three years. He was owned by a friend in York, who sold him to me just recently, so I had him brought down here. Fortunately he's settled well,' he supplied, rather haughtily.

'Fortunate, too, that Ann Vernon could take him. Which is his box?' Kate asked.

'The one by the tack-room, which suits him as he

likes to see folk passing by. Most stop and speak to him, which he likes even more. Which horse are you hiring today, or do you own your own?' he enquired, his dark gaze roaming round the yard.

'No, I don't own one. No such luck.' Kate stepped back from Hercules. 'But Ann tries to keep Cascade free for me—that's the mare with the light-coloured mane, down at the far end.'

'Ah, yes.' Following her pointing arm, Lucas nodded. 'The little palomino. Very suitable!'

Something about the way he said this made Kate's hackles rise. Plainly he thought she was capable of riding only the mildest of mounts. 'I've also ridden Raja, the bay stallion, when Cascade wasn't free. He's very suitable too.' She made her point with care.

'Splendid!' Lucas was looking amused, and, furious with herself for letting him get to her, Kate was relieved to see Iris approaching, leading Cascade.

A short, sturdy girl, she smiled fulsomely at both Kate and Lucas, keeping Cascade well back from the stallion. 'I swear she knows when it's Saturday, Miss Maybury.' Iris laughed as the little mare nudged Kate's shoulder and nickered into her hand.

'Good Cassie, good girl!' Kate took the reins.

Lucas called 'Enjoy your ride!' over his shoulder and led Hercules away.

Kate was glad he wasn't there when she mounted for, however adept, hoisting oneself into the saddle—especially for a woman—wasn't the most elegant sight in the world. And he'd be gone when she got back, thank goodness. Adjusting her riding hat, she set off into the dull, rather gloomy afternoon, breaking into a trot once she was clear of the yard.

Thoughts of Lucas filled her mind during the first

half-mile, which was annoying because she'd been all but oblivious of the straight ride along Loamers Lane, which she always enjoyed. He was unsettling, she decided, a disturbing man. He stayed in her mind like a burr that wouldn't be dislodged. Even so, she did her best to oust him, concentrating instead on the thrill of being in the saddle again, of consciously relaxing her shoulders and hips to absorb the cantering motion. It was bliss, the horse between her knees, the wind in her face parting to receive her, folding behind like wings, Cascade's hooves—muted and rhythmic—sending up clods of turf.

When she reached Fenton Wood she walked the mare through it then turned back to ride down the heath to where the town lay shrouded in mist, back to the yard, where she handed Cascade over to Iris to be unsaddled and rubbed down. She would have liked to have done this task herself, she usually did, but at half past five she was driving into Seftonbridge to meet her mother off the London train. 'See you soon, Cassie!' Leaning her cheek briefly against the horse's neck, she stood for a moment or two watching her being led away.

Because of the dull misty afternoon the lights were on in the yard. Hercules's box was next to the tackroom, she recalled, and on her way there to leave her hat, she looked in on him, curious to see him again. He was busy with his hay net, standing well back, showing clear signs that he didn't want to be bothered with a load of chat. Even so, Kate called out to him, telling him what a gorgeous hunk he was. 'Arrogant, though, and conceited, exactly like your boss. Probably with his manners as well, which isn't saying much!' Hercules ignored her, turning round so that all she could see was his rump. 'I rest my case.' She chuckled, moving along to the tack-room, where the light was on, where Lucas—oh, please, no—was immersing stirrups in a bucket, shirtsleeves rolled up.

She gasped audibly, caught her breath, very nearly choked. 'You startled me. I didn't expect… I thought you'd have gone by now.'

'Not quite yet.' He looked up and smiled. 'Had a good ride?' he asked.

'Yes, thanks.' Kate's head whirled. Had he heard what she'd said? Had he heard? He might not have done. There'd been other sounds in the yard, he might have heard the sound of her voice, but nothing distinct. Gaining courage, for he was looking unfazed, she decided to find out for sure. 'I've been having a word with Hercules,' she told him, wrenching off her hat.

'I know, I heard you.' He let her absorb that, then added silkily, 'But I'm sorry you think he's conceited. He's quite a modest fellow when you get to know him properly!'

'Oh, well, yes, I'm sure…' The whole of Kate's body went hot.

'And his manners, on the whole, are really very good. As for being arrogant, well, that, too, is a little unfair, I think.'

'You heard, didn't you?' Kate's heart thumped.

'I'm afraid so, yes.' Lucas had the stirrups out of the bucket now and was rubbing them up to a shine, his shadow huge on the wall behind him, cutting Kate down to size.

'Well, you know what they say about eavesdroppers.' She tried to laugh and failed. He ignored her and just carried on with his cleaning, giving the saddle and bridle special attention with saddle-soap.

'You don't have to clean your own tack. Iris would do it,' Kate said unwisely, digging for a reaction of *some* sort, at any rate.

He looked up then, meeting her gaze across the bench. 'I know, and she offered.' His voice was clipped. 'But I prefer to do it myself. You've no quarrel with that, I hope?' His slate-grey eyes were like stones, and just for a second she blenched.

'No, of course not,' she said, but a quarrel was brewing, she could feel it zinging between them. What she'd said out in the yard had been rude, not rude to his face but indirectly so, and certainly rude now he'd heard. It wasn't even entirely true either, for he wasn't a mannerless man. 'I'm sorry,' she said, and her words came out baldly, but she couldn't add to them.

'Sorry I heard... Yes, I dare say you are,' was his unforgiving response. He was hanging up the saddle and bridle, turning his back on her. He didn't seem in any hurry to turn round again either.

Perhaps he was waiting for her to abase herself properly. Well, if he is, tough, Kate thought, giving him the widest possible berth as she crossed the room to slam her hat on its peg. She said goodnight to him, she allowed herself that, but in her haste to get out of the door she didn't watch where she was putting her feet, didn't see the open tin of saddle-soap which had fallen onto the floor. The next second her heel was in it, her leg was shooting out and with a crash and a cry she was flat on her back, narrowly missing the bucket of water, which she stared at dazedly as she rolled to pick herself up.

'*Kate!*' He was beside her in seconds, lifting her to her feet. 'Kate, are you hurt?' He supported her, holding her back from him slightly, his hands at her waist as his eyes ran over her. Then he touched the back of her head. 'Are you hurt?' he repeated, and she felt the puff of his breath against her cheek.

'No, I'm not…no thanks to you.' To be angry helped. Better that than to cry in front of him. 'What a daft place to leave soap. Couldn't you have put it back on the bench?'

'I wasn't expecting a visitor, was I?' His voice was very soft. He hadn't missed the blinked-away tears, or the pallor of her face. 'I really am so very sorry,' he said as she moved carefully away from him, testing the state of her legs. Her behind hurt, and she longed to rub it, but couldn't do so with him standing in front of her, watching her like a hawk. And to make matters worse, he was sitting her down on a rock-hard stool.

'I'm all right, I don't need…' she began, but he took no notice. Then, squatting in front of her and raising her 'skid' leg, he painstakingly cleaned every vestige of saddle-soap from the heel of her boot. Cautioning her to stay where she was and still keeping an eye on her, he reached for his jacket and buttoned it, standing a mere matter of inches in front of her, and talked about running her home.

Fast recovering from one shock, Kate was now fighting another, battling against a surge of feelings aroused by his nearness. His flat, cream jodhpur'd front became the extent of her vision, his male scent, combined with the tweedy reek of his jacket, drew her like nothing else. What she wanted was to feel him against her, to have him hold her and press her close, yet when his hand came under her elbow to help her up, she all but flung it off. He took scant notice, just gripped it more tightly. 'Kate, let me drive you home!'

'There's no need. I'm perfectly all right!' She looked fixedly at the open door.

'Are you quite sure?' He let go of her arm, moving back from her at last. 'You came down with one hell of a bump, you know.'

'You're telling me!' With space between them, she was recovering fast. 'I came down with what my mother would call a fair whack. Still…' she turned in the doorway, fully in control once more '…I do have an unfortunate habit of slipping whenever there's something to do it on. I should have looked where I was going, shouldn't I? 'Night, then, and thanks.' And with that she stepped out into the lamplit yard, making for the far gate.

He watched her critically as she passed the yard buildings and stepped out into the open drive, relieved to see that she wasn't limping, or even moving slowly. In fact, she was literally striding out, head held high, a thick swirl of tawny hair hanging down her back. She didn't turn round or wave just before she passed from sight, not that he'd thought she would, of course, but the fact that she did not irked him and caused him to curse silently under his breath.

What was his horse like?' Kate's mother asked when they were gardening next day. She had been told about the meeting with Lucas, but not about the fall that had followed. Kate was keeping that to herself, but was nevertheless perfectly willing to expound on Hercules's finer points.

'Oh, he's black and massive, stands a good fifteen hands, I should think,' she replied, an annoying pang darting through her as she vizualised Lucas, high in the saddle, looking practically skyborne as he'd stared down at her.

Paula was waiting for more, but when nothing was forthcoming she began to talk about Lucas's father. 'He was an ophthalmic surgeon, apparently,' she began, clawing up a length of bramble, 'retired early, due to his arthritis, he's only in his mid-sixties now. Came here to Cletford two years ago to live in the cottage he and his wife used to spend the weekends in. She died of a coronary occlusion three or four years ago—he swears it was due to her worrying herself over him.'

'It's a wonder he hasn't been to the hospital for treatment before. I mean, if he's been here a couple of years...'

'He had private treatment at Seftonbridge at first, then once we opened the hydrotherapy pool at the Royal, he decided to switch.'

'Does he think it's doing him good?'

'Well, it undoubtedly *is*, whilst he's in the water. He's lonely, of course, although he'd never admit it, not in a thousand years. Still,' Paula continued, 'he's luckier than most, with his son not far off now and, plainly, he's comfortably off. He's not even all that disabled, he only uses one stick, manages to wash and dress himself, all that sort of thing.'

'What's he like as a person?' Kate enquired, not that she was all that interested, but her mother seemed to be, and this surprised her, for Paula was usually detached.

'We-ell...' She considered Kate's question. 'Inclined to be bloody-minded,' she said, 'but likable on his good days—a powerful man chafing at his chains is how I would describe him.'

Kate laughed, linking her arm in her mother's as they went back to the house. 'Take away the chains bit, and you've just given me a fair description of his son, Lucas!' she said.

CHAPTER THREE

WHEN Kate went on duty next morning she was greeted with the news that her colleague, Jean Bailey, had had an accident over the weekend. Sister Rooke, barely controlling her exasperation, called her into the office. 'She's had a skiing accident, of all things. She belongs to that dry-slope club over at Bartons End. Anyway, she fell, took a tumble, fractured her patella and she's down in Orthopaedics awaiting major surgery this morning.'

'Oh, I'm sorry to hear that,' Kate said, when she could get a word in.

'She'll be out of action for three months, probably more, just when we're stretched to breaking point.' Sister's chair scraped back on the vinyl floor as she moved to look up at Kate. 'What I want to know is if you can stay on, fill Jean's place. I've spoken to Miss Petersen, the SNO, who'll contact your agency—that is, if you're willing to take on a three months' stretch, and also, of course, providing you haven't got another assignment lined up.'

'No, I haven't,' Kate said, then hesitated as she took all this in. Did she really want to stay on here for that length of time? Her eyes swept the ward through the wide viewing window, taking in the twenty-eight surgical beds, all of them occupied, which meant hard and demanding work, skilful dedicated nursing with not enough back-up staff. Did she want that, for three months, here at Seftonbridge? Yes, she did, and she'd

39

make a success of it in spite of, or perhaps because of, Lucas, who'd raise his brows in disdain.

'You'd be acting in for me when I'm off duty,' Sister added, but whether she meant this as an inducement or a warning, Kate didn't know or care.

'I frequently had that kind of responsibility at St Mildred's,' she said, 'and I'd like to stay on.' She smiled as she said this, and Sister's tense face relaxed.

'Good. Well, I'll set the wheels in motion, then,' she said, and rang the bell for the rest of the shift to come in for the handover report.

'It is sad about Jean, isn't it?' Rose Liu, one of the quieter nurses, remarked to Kate when they were tidying beds a little later.

Kate, agreeing that it was, made a mental note to visit the orthopaedic unit during her lunchbreak. Jean would probably still be in Theatre, or in the recovery room, but even so she could get first-hand news of her, and also see Sandra Peck—that was, if she'd not been discharged. She wouldn't admit, not even to herself, that there was a third reason for giving up part of her lunch-break to make the trek over to Ortho, which was that she might catch a glimpse of Sister Claire Jevons, Lucas's girlfriend.

In the meantime, with four patients due for surgery right here in Guthrie Ward, the rest in stages of post-op recovery, not to mention the new admittances, the nurses were working at frenetic speed, passing from one job to the next, their heads full of a long list of things still to be done, whilst managing to maintain an atmosphere of calm so far as the patients were concerned. Kate, as she moved from one bed to another, from one job to another, reflected on what a pity it was that there was never time to talk to patients and get to know them better. There was scarcely time to allay their fears, although she made that a matter of priority, knowing how it felt to be in a hospital bed herself.

However, Mrs Benz, the hiatus hernia patient, who was second on this morning's list, displayed no nervous symptoms as Kate went through the list of checks before the theatre porters arrived.

With her upper denture in a pot on her locker, she smiled gappily up at Kate. 'I'm what my young granddaughter would call cool, Nurse, which means calm. I shan't be sorry when it's all over, though, and my inside is behaving itself. I can't even lie comfortably in bed unless I'm practically propped up on end!'

'That must be awful,' Kate sympathised, whilst checking her patient's identity band and making sure her consent form was signed.

'The dark-haired doctor, the one with the eyebrows, says I've nothing to worry about. He's going to sew up the gap so as to stop food shooting up into my chest.'

'You'll be fine afterwards, so much better.'

'I'm glad he's doing it, he'll make a good job of it. Seems to me…' Drowsy from the premed, Mrs Benz tried to wink. 'Seems to me he'd be good at most things, don't you agree with me, dear?'

Kate did, and agreed aloud, but that was all she said for the porters were coming in with their trolley, and off Mrs Benz went, raising a feeble but still gallant hand to the occupants of the six beds she passed on her way to the doors.

'Makes you feel funny, seeing them go off,' Miss Dawes, the new goitre patient, called out to Kate, who stopped checking notes at the ward desk and went over to speak to her. Kate recognised a nervous patient when she saw one, realising, too, that Emily Dawes's thyroid condition didn't help her jittery state.

'Is this your first time in hospital?' she asked, and was told it was. Commiserating with her, Kate tried her best to calm the woman's fears. She would have liked to have pulled out a chair and sat down with her, but couldn't neglect other patients to do so. Mondays on surgical wards were horrendous—the worst day of the week.

Shortly before midday Peter Graves arrived to see June Tredgold, and Sister asked Kate to accompany him into the side-ward as she was engaged with the SNO. It was five days since June's partial gastrectomy, and she had progressed well, so much so that Peter was able to tell her she could come off parenteral feeding. 'Oh, good,' she said, 'just in time for lunch, and what I *really* fancy…' she smiled at Peter '…is a plate of fish and chips!'

'In your dreams,' he said, grinning back. 'It'll be soup for you today, then tomorrow, maybe, a little steamed fish. We're not absolutely home and dry yet, you know!'

June continued to look radiant. 'Bernie will be pleased when he visits this afternoon. He hated these tubes.' She looked down at the one running into her arm. 'He thought they meant I was at death's door! So, when—' she looked enquiringly at Kate '—will you take them out?'

'Just as soon as I've seen Dr Graves off the premises,' Kate told her, laughing.

'It's Peter,' he said, looking closely at her as they emerged into the corridor. 'I've just heard you're staying with us for the next few weeks, so we'll begin as we mean to go on.'

'Of course, and I'm Kate, and I'm glad to be staying, but I'm sorry about Jean,' she added, remembering that Jean and Peter had seemed to get on well.

'Yes, it's very bad luck.' His chunky face looked concerned. 'The trouble about major knee surgery is that it disables one for weeks and for a nurse, who has to be on her feet a lot, it means a long convalescence. Still, it's fortunate that you can stay on with us. I, for one, am glad about that.' He smiled at her, then called out, 'See you soon,' before he pushed through the corridor doors.

Kate was left with the pleasant feeling of having been welcomed and her step was light as she went into the ward. Summoning Karen, she asked her to lay up a trolley in Clean Utility... 'Then take it to the side-ward where you can help me take out June's gastric tube and drip.'

The girl went off, the job was completed and, with soup ordered for June's lunch, Kate liaised with Sister over the roster for the following week. After that came the ritual of ward lunches, following which Kate bought a sandwich at the hospital shop, then took herself over to the orthopaedic wing and up to Docherty Ward.

As she thought would be the case, Jean was still in Recovery, but her operation had gone well. 'She should be back here within the hour,' Sister Jevons told Kate, coming out of her office when she saw a strange nurse arrive.

She was small, blonde, curvy and attractive, this girl-friend of Lucas Brown's. Kate took a good smiling look at her, trying to pinpoint her age. Claire Jevons, in her turn, was running her eyes over Kate.

'You're the agency nurse from Guthrie, aren't you?'

She gave a small closed smile. 'I've been hearing all good things about you. News round here travels fast.'

It must, Kate was thinking, and where did it stem from? Not from Lucas, that was for sure. 'Chloe Rooke,' Claire was saying, unconsciously answering Kate's unspoken question, 'is thrilled out of her socks to get a nurse of your calibre.'

'Well, for my part, I'm thrilled to get a long placement, especially on a surgical ward, although I'm sorry Jean had to fracture a kneecap to bring that about.' Kate sounded acerbic, and knew she did, but having so many compliments thrown at her by someone she'd only just met made her feel more than a little uncomfortable.

'It just takes time to heal, that's all.' Claire glanced back into her office at this point and, taking the hint, Kate asked if she could go into the ward to see Sandra Peck. 'She was with us for two days on Guthrie, as you know, and I promised I'd look her up.'

'Of course, that's fine. She's halfway up on the right-hand side, but keep it brief—it's the quiet hour.' With this little assertion of her rank Sister Jevons swept into her room.

The ward looked untidy, but this was a facet of ortho wards. Kate made her way past dozing patients, most with a limb in plaster strung up on a frame. One young woman was on pelvis traction, lying flat with a pulley arrangement and weights at the end of her bed. She was reading with difficulty and smiled at Kate as she passed.

Sandra was still finding it difficult to smile, but she was pleased to see Kate. Her nose was in a splint, her nostrils packed with gauze. 'I know I look a fearful sight.' She motioned to Kate to sit down. 'But Jim, my boyfriend, came in last night, and he managed not to faint.'

'Oh, good for him!' Kate laughed, glad that Sandra could joke.

'I feel better since he's been. He didn't seem too appalled, just concerned for me, you know. It's brought us closer, not the other way round.'

'I think I know what you mean.'

'I can turn to him.'

'That's everything, I know.' Kate stifled a sigh.

'And I feel I can face the others now, which is just as well as three of our mates—we live in a student house—are coming in tonight. I *may* be rid of this in a week.' She touched the plaster splint. 'Then I'll need to get my tooth fixed. Jim's father is a dentist in Cletford, so he'll help me with that.'

'Better and better!' Kate smiled, and was just about to ask Sandra if her bicycle had been taken care of when Claire Jevons appeared at the ward doors, indicating that she would like Sandra's visitor to get back to her own ward.

So off Kate went, aware as she sped down the long corridor that Claire was one of those people who could convey a message without saying a word. Was Lucas in love with her? she wondered. He might well be, she was very much the type men went for—small, blonde, neat and curvaceous, with lashes to die for. Need one say more? she conjectured ruefully, catching sight of her own long leanness in the glass of the corridor doors.

She was on the late shift next day—working from twelve-thirty to nine at night. This meant that, with Chloe Rooke going off at half past four, she, Kate, was in charge. She told herself that it was no big deal and that she was fully capable of dealing with anything that might arise. Even so, watching Chloe's broad back disappearing up the corridor with the rest of the earlies shift, she had one or two anxiety twinges in the shape of butterflies.

She did a quick round of the ward first, which still had one or two visitors, then, checking with the nurses at the ward desk, she returned to the office to make a start on the inevitable paperwork. She had read somewhere that a ward sister, in carrying out her duties, could expect to be interrupted every six or seven minutes. This, Kate found, was certainly the case over the next two hours. First came a tap on the door and in came a florid-faced visitor, the mother of one of the hernia patients, complaining that her daughter wasn't getting her 'proper eggs'.

'I brought her in half a dozen free-range ones, marked with a little green circle that I drew on myself, but she tells me she's never had one of them, only little white pullet-sized ones. She's not one to complain, so I'm doing it for her. I mean, it doesn't seem right that other people should have my Madge's eggs.'

'No, it doesn't, Mrs Driver, I'll look into it, I promise!' Kate wrote, 'Eggs, green circle,' on the pad beside her phone.

'Can't she keep them in her locker?' Mrs Driver inched nearer to the desk. 'Then she could just hand one out to you when she wants one boiled?'

'I'll look into it, I promise,' Kate repeated, relieved and reprieved when her phone rang and Mrs Driver went out. Not that the caller on the other end of the phone gave her much joy, for it was the laundry manager, complaining about bags again. 'You've been overfilling them, the consequence being we've had stinking, horrible sheets flowing out all over the place!'

'I'm so sorry, I'll see that it doesn't happen again.' Kate added 'laundry bags' to her list, just as the husband of one of the stoma patients came in all flustered and worried about his wife. 'She says she's changed her mind about going convalescent, Sister, says she'd rather come straight home from here and have the district nurse call. I'm not happy about it, not happy at all. I mean, of course I want her home, but I'm nervous about that stoma thing, and the district nurse won't be able to be with us all the time, will she?'

The poor man looked close to tears, and Kate felt sorry for him. 'I'll ask one of the doctors to have a word with Mrs Joley.' Kate was recalling the case—an ileostomy after a long weakening period of ulcerative colitis. 'She's Mr Brown's patient, isn't she? He will tell her exactly what's involved in her after-care. I know he thought convalescence in a nursing home would be the best course, and he may be able to talk your wife round.'

Mr Joley went off, muttering something to the effect that his Mavis was a right stubborn woman. Kate returned to her paperwork, but was soon interrupted by a haughty young woman in designer glasses. She came in without knocking, announcing that she was from Sterile Central Supply and asking whether her stock sheets were ready.

'No,' Kate said firmly, 'they aren't, I've not made a start on them yet. I'll ring through and let you know when they're done. They're next on my list.'

'Oh, right. You're new, aren't you? Agency, I see!' The last was a little dig, which Kate ignored, and the woman went off with her sharp chin thrust forward, making a clacking noise with her heels.

'CSSD Sheets' went down on Kate's list, then in came Zelda with a cup of tea, which she gulped down as she worked. In the ward beds were being tidied after visitors, flowers were being brought out, walking patients were shuffling to the loos, the less able helped onto commodes. All too soon it was suppertime, then visitors again. June Tredgold's husband looked in on Kate, sweating profusely, saying that June was asleep and ought he to wake her up? His anxiety was obvious and Kate felt sorry for him. 'Well, you can,' she said, 'but why not just sit with her for a minute or two and see if she wakes naturally? If she doesn't, then by all means wake her, she'll want to know you've come.'

'Yes, I'll do that, thank you, Nurse.' He went off to the side-ward, pushing against the tide of visitors coming in from the lifts.

Evening visitors were mostly working people who couldn't manage to visit in the afternoons. Often they wanted a word with the nurse on duty, so when Kate, with her back to the door as she stood at the filing cabinet, heard someone come in, she assumed it was a worried or complaining relative and was startled to see Lucas standing in the doorway! What on earth did he want? There was no emergency. Had it gone seven o'clock? All this chased through her head, whilst the words 'Oh, *no*!' escaped her lips before she could bite them back.

'Not very welcoming!' His expression was wry, whilst a small smile teased the corners of his mouth. 'Plainly,' he said, his eyes taking in the pile of work on the desk, 'I've come at a bad time, but all I want is Brenda Smith's notes. As you're right at the cabinet, perhaps you could get them out for me?'

'Yes, of course.' Through a blur of embarrassment, Kate handed him Miss Smith's notes, then made to walk with him into the ward. He stopped her, saying that it wasn't necessary.

'I'm not going to examine her, just talk to her about her chemotherapy.'

'Oh, yes, of course. I'm sorry!' Kate sat down again, feeling thrown and disconcerted and in the wrong, sensations that came so easily to the fore whenever he was around. She should have gone into the ward with him. Chloe would have done. He was a senior registrar, for goodness' sake, so what was she thinking of? But her discomfiture was by no means finished, for within seconds he was back, moving behind her chair and laying the folder of notes on her desk.

'People with common names are a damn nuisance, aren't they, Sister?'

Kate saw what he meant—she knew what she'd done, even before he'd finished speaking. The name on the tab of the file was 'Smith, Audrey'. She had given him the wrong notes.

'I'm so sorry!' She made to get up, but his hand clamped down on her shoulder and anchored her to her seat.

'This time I'll help myself,' he said shortly, and proceeded to do just that, whisking behind her as he went out, making a little draught.

Mortified, furious with herself, Kate tried to settle again, but she had scarcely taken up her pen when a cry that was very nearly a shriek echoed from the side-ward. Almost simultaneously its summoning bell shrilled on the board outside. What on earth…? Kate

tore up the corridor, Nurse Liu at her heels. The side-
ward door was open and there, on the floor, was the
prone figure of Bernard Tredgold, June half-crouched
at his side.

'Help me turn him!' Kate snapped at Rose Liu, as
she felt for a pulse. There was none. He'd arrested.
'Ring Resus. *Fast!*' She started cardiac massage, counting as she did so. Ten depressions, then she breathed
slowly full into his mouth, blocking his nostrils with
one hand.

Someone had called Lucas. Kate saw him come in
when she moved to begin cardiac massage again. 'Let
me help,' he said, and thankfully she let him, and seconds later they heard the unmistakable sound of the
resuscitation trolley being whirled down the corridor.

The team took over. Lucas, Kate and Rose Liu, with
June in a wheelchair, left them to it at their request,
for there was scant room for manoeuvre in a relatively
small room. June, warmly wrapped, was wheeled into
the office with Lucas and Kate. She needed their company, whilst they needed to know exactly what had
happened.

'Will he be all right? Is he going to be all right?'
She was incoherent at first, refusing the warm milk
Kate had brought in for her.

'They'll do everything they can, he's in expert
hands,' Lucas assured her, but she carried on talking
as though he'd not spoken.

'I thought he was asleep at first. I'd been dozing,
and I woke up and saw him, sitting there in the chair,
I thought he was asleep, but when I spoke he didn't
answer, and when I got out of bed and touched him he
fell forward onto his face!'

Kate and Lucas exchanged covert glances, each of

them thinking the same—that it was highly likely that by the time June had awakened from her doze Bernard hadn't been breathing for several minutes, maybe as many as five. Kate felt her mouth go dry.

'He shouldn't have come.' June was still talking. 'It's too much for him in an evening. He's been over-working, having chest pains, our doctor was sending him for tests!' She was crying now and the jerking hurt her wound. Kate put an arm round her shoulders just as the door opened and the red-haired anaesthetist who'd headed the resus team beckoned to Lucas, who joined him in the corridor. 'That means he's dead. He's dead! I know it!' June's eyes were on the closed door and Kate had to forcibly restrain her from getting out of the wheelchair.

'June, we don't know,' she began. Then the two men came back.

'He's dead, isn't he?' June's eyes were on Lucas, who sat down and took her hand.

'Yes,' he said simply, whilst the red-haired young doctor went on to explain that even if he'd been able to resuscitate Bernard, he would have been severely brain-damaged.

June was belligerent. 'I want to see him *now*!' she said, looking at Lucas again.

So he took her along, leaving Kate to deal with the aftermath of a visitor dying suddenly on the ward.

June was transferred to the second of the two side-wards and given a sedative. The senior nursing officer was informed and came down when the police arrived, Lucas and Kate being present when the latter questioned June. By then she had telephoned her mother in London and spoken to Bernard's parents, waving aside Kate's suggestion that she should wait until morning.

In the ward the medicine round was in progress, supervised by Nurse Beck. The last of the visitors had gone, for it was nearly nine o'clock. Kate could hear the activity of bedtime drinks being handed around as she wrote up the nursing report. Rose Liu was sitting with June until she fell into a drugged sleep. As for Lucas, he had gone off with the SNO over half an hour ago. He might at least have said goodnight, Kate was thinking, blowing a strand of hair off her hot, sticky face. It had been a terrible shift with a shocking ending. Small wonder she felt shattered. Yet, despite her weariness, despite the fact that she hadn't eaten for hours, despite the vision of a dozen different faces sailing past her like ghosts, she felt she hadn't done too badly. She felt she had coped, apart from that business of sending Lucas into the ward with the wrong set of notes!

Kate knew the night nurses had arrived when she heard the thud of the corridor doors and heard the staff go into the locker-room. A while later one trained nurse and one auxiliary appeared at her door, ready to start work. Once the hand-over report was done Kate emphasised the need to keep a special eye on June. 'She'll still be in shock,' she said.

'We'll do our best, but with only two of us on...' The staff nurse raised expressive brows, looking even more put about when Kate said, surprising herself, 'I could stay on for a bit, say a couple of hours, if that would help.'

It was then that into the astonished, rather frigid silence a voice in the corridor spoke. 'If you've a couple of hours to spare, Nurse Maybury, I wonder if you could do me a favour?'

'Why, yes, if I can.' Kate turned round to see Lucas framed in the doorway, his white coat hanging loosely.

'Is it to do with June? I was just saying to Nurse here—'

'No, it isn't.' he cut her off in mid-sentence. 'June Tredgold is now in the care of the night staff, so if you could come with me, please…' He practically wafted her from the room, nodding goodnight to a gaping Nurse Linton, who clearly wondered what was going on. And so, for that matter, did Kate.

'Why on earth,' he asked out in the corridor, 'did you offer to stay on? No one is indispensable, and I should think—by the look of you—that you've had enough for one day.'

Kate bridled a little. What exactly did he mean by that? He was impossible…so dictatorial! 'Neither you nor I,' he continued, 'can do any more for June tonight. All she needs is an eye kept on her, and the night staff are capable of that. Peter Graves is on call, and he's been put in the picture. We're not absconding or leaving anything to chance.'

The 'we' sounded cosy. She began to melt a little, and to wonder, even more, what he wanted of her. They had reached the door leading to the staff cloakrooms and he told her to go and get her coat. 'Then would you meet me on the forecourt outside A and E? I thought we could go out and have something to eat.'

'Out… Eat?' She gaped at him.

'It's called supper.' He was stripping off his white coat, hanging it over his arm. 'We're both in desperate need of sustenance, so go and get your coat,' he repeated with emphasis, opening the door for her.

Standing in front of the line of washbasins, Kate still had the stunned sensation of having been hit on the head. Perhaps, she thought, face-to-face with herself in the mirror, he sees me as less of a pain now, or simply wants someone to eat with, or is at some sort of loose end.

She smoothed a cleansing wipe over her face and dealt with a few wisps of hair then, applying a trace of lip gloss, reached for her jacket. Her hands were shaking slightly so she had trouble doing up the zip, which she put down to exhaustion. It had *nothing* to do with Lucas! she told herself.

Even so, five minutes later, seeing him waiting for her under the brilliance of A and E's lights, she couldn't deny the little stir of pleasure she felt in her stomach. As they walked towards one another she melted some more. But she had to be careful, she warned herself. She mustn't let down her guard.

He took Kate's arm, smiling at her. 'I've rung for a taxi,' he said. 'I thought taking two cars into the town centre at this time of night, and hoping to park, would be asking too much of fate.'

'We could have walked!'

'I don't think so... Ah, here's our cab!' It swung into the kerb. 'Bellini's,' he called to the driver as he helped Kate in, slipping in beside her and slamming the door. 'I'm assuming,' he said as they joined the traffic in the town, 'that you like Italian food?'

'Yes, I do, very much,' she replied, and thought how stilted she sounded. Shyness was something that seldom affected her, but she was feeling it with Lucas in this different and confined environment, breathing the same air as him.

Seftonbridge had lots of Italian restaurants, but Bellini's, though smaller than some, was the oldest, most established and the most upmarket, situated in the bustling heart of the university town.

Sitting opposite Lucas at one of its snowy-clothed tables a few minutes later, watching their plates of prawn pasta and bowls of green salad being placed in front of them, Kate began to relax, glad that she'd come. She suddenly felt really hungry.

'When did you last eat?' Lucas asked, winding spaghetti round his fork with enviable expertise.

'Oh, I had a sandwich at some point,' she told him. 'I can't remember exactly when.'

'It was one crisis after another, wasn't it?'

'You can say that again,' she said soberly, her mind flicking back to that awful business of June's husband. She wished Lucas wouldn't talk shop.

It seemed he intended to do so, though. 'Chloe Rooke,' he said, 'couldn't have coped or kept her head any better than you did this afternoon, and she's a real pro with years of management under her belt.'

Startled, Kate looked at him. Was he sending her up? He didn't seem to be, his slate-grey eyes, as they locked with hers, held no trace of mockery. 'Thanks for saying that.' Her voice shook.

'I only speak the truth!' He smiled at her then and she at him, and as their glances held she had the feeling that he'd thrown her a lifeline and was drawing her close to him. It ended, of course, with him looking away and gulping water from his glass. 'What I can't understand,' he said abruptly and gruffly, 'is why someone with your considerable experience should give up a senior nursing post in Town and come back here to take up agency work.'

'Do we have to talk shop?'

'For the moment, yes.' He was giving her no choice. She looked down at her place, wondering whether to come clean or not. She didn't have to, she could just tell him part of the reason and leave it at that. In the end she decided to recount the full story. It was possible, anyway, that her mother in one of her chats with Lucas's father would say something about it, so Lucas might as well hear it now.

'A long-term relationship I was in petered out,' she began, 'so that was one reason, but there was another horrible one.' She faltered then went doggedly on, 'I was mugged one night on the way home, after a late shift.'

'Oh, my God!' Lucas's voice throbbed. 'Were you…? How did…?'

'My arm was dislocated. I tried to hold on to my bag, but I was shaken and pulled and the back of my head was introduced to a wall!'

'Kate!'

'I had three broken ribs and mild concussion and I was in hospital for a time. It was fortunate that another nurse found me, so I got treatment fast.'

'When did this happen?'

'Last March. I went home to recover after I left hospital. When I was fit, and it didn't take all that long, I went back to London to complete my contract, which only had three months to run. I was sure I'd want to sign on again, that I'd be cool about it all, but I couldn't settle, so at my mother's suggestion I came home and registered with the agency. The rest you know.'

'Were you able to give a description to the police— of who attacked you, I mean?'

'No, I didn't really get a proper look at him, it all

happened so fast. He was thickset, with a beard, and had a horrible smell. I can sometimes smell him now!'

A gasp or growl escaped Lucas. He put out a hand as if to grasp hers over the tabletop, then he drew it quickly back, splashing more water into his glass, glaring at it in disgust. 'What I wouldn't give to change this into a brandy for each of us!'

'No chance. We'll both be behind steering-wheels pretty soon!' Kate was feeling better, even gratified, for he'd minded about her attack. The appalled look still sat on his face. He hadn't just said, 'Oh, how terrible,' and pretended the rest. He hadn't asked—as Clive, her boyfriend, had—if she'd got her bag back. She hadn't, but in retrospect the bag didn't matter, even though she'd fought like a tigress for it at the time. And if it *had* been found, she knew she'd never have been able to touch it again.

'We needn't go home just yet.' Lucas was looking round for their waiter. 'We'll have some coffee—a pot, not a cup—then we can both relax.'

'And talk of pleasant, ordinary happenings?'

'Absolutely!' Lucas smiled at her and she felt her insides melt again.

The coffee, when it came, was Bellini's best—scaldingly hot and strong. 'Black as the devil and sweet as love, as my grandfather used to say!' Lucas said with lashes downcast, spooning sugar into his cup.

So he could flirt, could he? Kate's heart thumped. 'Which is just how I like it,' she countered, playing up.

It was when they were on their second cup that he asked who had taught her to ride. 'Oh, my father,' she

told him. 'Ten years ago when I got my A-level re-
sults.'

'Did *he* ride?'

'He did, yes, he was a firm believer in exercise. He
died when I was in my second year of training.'

'What of?' She had Lucas's full attention.

'Pneumonia after flu. It was incredibly quick. My
mother was traumatised, we both were,' she said.

'It's a terrible thing to lose a parent, whatever age
one is. It's especially terrible for the one who's left.
Good thing your mother had her career. Work does
help,' Lucas said reflectively, turning his cup round and
round.

'My mother's always worked,' Kate told him. 'Both
she and my father were always out of the house by
nine every weekday morning. I was mostly looked after
by au pairs. Not that I minded that, they were good
fun, most of them, we had a new one every year. Dad
used to mimic their accents, but they took it all in good
part. He was a dentist in East Road and had the practice
Hurst and Rodgers run now.'

'I know it, I go to them.' Lucas's tongue investigated
a troublesome molar he'd just had filled. 'Were you,'
he went on, 'educated in Seftonbridge?'

'Oh, yes, at The Rotyngs. I expect you went to
boarding school?'

'I did, but as a day boy.'

'Then to university here?'

'No, Durham. My family were all in the north then,
and we were pretty close-knit. Dad didn't move down
here till just on two years ago. He felt the milder south
would be more kind to him healthwise, although at this

time of year the mist and colder temperatures don't do much for him.'

The mist was very much in evidence when some fifteen minutes later they left the restaurant and set off on foot for the hospital. Lucas wanted to ring for a taxi, but Kate was all for walking. 'It's not far, and swanning around in taxis is such a waste.'

'A bit decadent, you mean?' He was helping her into her jacket.

'More lazy!' she retorted, and he laughed out loud, watching her tip her hood forward over her tawny gold hair.

He slipped a hand through her arm, 'Right, then, off we go into the murk!' Not that it was really murky, there was too much street lighting for that, but a thin mist was blowing in from the river, and as they turned into Princes Parade the lamps in ancient doorways and courtyards had an elongated, shrouded appearance, like waiting, watching ghosts.

But apparitions and an eerie atmosphere were lost on Kate. She was conscious only of the warm, breathing, flesh-and-blood male at her side. By just flicking her eyes Kate could see his face not so far from her own, see his ear and the angle of his jaw, his nose and one half of his mouth. She shivered and he asked her if she was cold.

'A little,' she lied.

'We should have had that taxi.'

'Nonsense. We're nearly there,' she said, as the hospital buildings came into view. 'What I would like,' she went on as they approached the nearest entrance, 'is a small flat, or a room in the town, now that I know I'm going to be here for the next three months.'

'With the academic year only just starting, you'll have difficulty,' Lucas observed. 'Every room, every cupboard and cranny in Seftonbridge will be let out to students.' When in sight of her car he released her arm so that she could dive into her bag for her keys. 'I suppose you had your own place in London?' he asked.

'Yes, a flat in Borough High Street.' For some reason Kate didn't add that it was the flat she and Clive had shared, even though Lucas seemed to be waiting for her to tell him more.

When she didn't he held out his hand for her keys and bent to unlock her car door. He held it wide for her to slip in, then said, as she squeezed past him, 'I would have thought with your own transport, and with Cletford relatively close, it would be better to carry on as you are. Even tranquil Seftonbridge has its share of thieves and vagabonds!'

'You wouldn't be worrying about me, by any chance, would you?' Kate gave a little grimace, as she climbed in.

'A little.' He was serious-faced and looked at her intently.

Kate laughed and flipped back her head. 'For goodness' sake, Lucas, being mugged in London hasn't got me running scared, and surely you've heard the saying that lightning seldom strikes the same place twice.'

He made a sound like a grunt and swooped down, taking her by surprise, taking her mouth with efficient ease, cupping the back of her head with his hand. His lips were closed and warm over hers, then she felt the trail of his breath upwards over her cheeks and forehead as he straightened and moved away.

'Drive carefully.' The words came through the half-open door.

'I will, and…thanks.'

He smiled, clicked the door shut and moved back, leaving her to move slowly forward towards the exit gates.

The kiss stayed in Kate's mind all the way home, and she wondered why. It hadn't been fiercely passionate, or demanding. It had just been a goodnight kiss, so why had it filled her up to the brim and caused such a rush of delight?

CHAPTER FOUR

'YOU can rent my flat if you like. I'm not likely to be wanting it for the next three months.' Jean stared gloomily at the long cast encasing her right leg.

It was the following evening and Kate, in the role of visitor, had been giving Jean all the news of the ward, including yesterday's shocking happening and how June Tredgold was bearing up. She didn't mention her supper with Lucas, for that was private business, but she did let on that she would like to find temporary living accommodation in the town, so when Jean made her suggestion she jumped to at once.

'Do you mean it, Jean? Are you serious?' She tried not to sound too eager, but to remember how Jean must be feeling.

'Of course I mean it.' Jean sniffed. 'I wouldn't mention it otherwise. I've got it on a three-year lease, but I'm allowed to sub-let. It's up the road here, in Bridge Street, in that small parade of shops running down to the river. It's over Lew's, the greengrocer's...you must know where I mean.'

'Yes, I do. I used to shop there when I was training. The greengrocer's was Chadwick's then.' Kate was more than interested now. Bridge Street was very near.

'Well, I don't know about that, but it's Lew's now. He's a decent enough bloke, lets me have my fruit and veg cheap and carries it up to the flat. He'd be tickled pink to have another nurse living over the shop, he always said I made him feel safe in case he had a funny turn in the shop!' Tears of weakness began to roll down Jean's pale face. She was only on her second post-op day and couldn't stand very much. Seeing this and feeling guilty, Kate got to her feet. 'We'll talk about it at another time, Jean, I'm wearing you out.'

Jean shook her head and mopped up, shifting her leg on the bed. 'You may as well get the keys out of my bag, and go and have a look.' She dragged her bag out of her locker and thrust it at Kate, just as Claire appeared at the ward doors, Lucas at her side, ringed by a straggle of evening visitors.

'Crikey, look who's come.' Jean roused herself. 'I bet he's paying a visit to Sandra Peck, lucky so and so!'

It seemed as though she was right, too, for the duo were making their way to the far end of the ward, where Sandra, who was entertaining a spotty youth, was sitting out of bed. 'Well, she *is* his one-time patient,' Kate said.

'Yeah, right.' Jean looked disgruntled.

'He's probably just come up from Theatre. We had an emergency appendix brought in at four o'clock.' Kate's mouth was dry and her hands were shaking as she groped in Jean's bag for the keys. For pity's sake— she tried to calm down—he won't be coming up here.

'What's Sandra Peck got that I haven't? What's a nose compared to a leg?' Jean's normal good humour was asserting itself as she went on to tell Kate that the larger of the two keys opened the street door at the side of the shop, whilst the smaller one opened the flat. She handed both over, then gave a small jerk as she glanced down the ward again. 'Look, Kate, they're coming over here!'

She was right, they were, and making good progress,

speaking to other patients on the way, Claire's blond head scarcely reaching Lucas's blue-shirted shoulder. He had probably, Kate thought, dressed in a hurry after Theatre and forgotten to pick his jacket up. As they reached the bed, she stood up, giving him room to pass. 'There now, you already have a visitor and don't need another!' he joked, smiling at both women and asking Jean how she was feeling. 'Not in too much pain, I hope?'

'It comes and goes, but not a lot,' she said, her face going pink in patches. 'But of all the stupid things to do, Mr Brown. Now I'm out of action for ages!'

'All accidents are stupid, Jean. When we've had one we always think how easily it could have been avoided. You must know what I mean—that "if only" thing.' His smile included Kate as he said this, and she wondered if he was thinking about her own 'accident' in London.

'Nice of you to come to see me.' Jean was holding full court.

'Oh, I meant to do so, if only to tell you how much you're missed on the ward.'

'Good of you to say so.' Jean looked fretfully down at her plaster again. 'But Kate can do my job equally well, and they're getting a junior in. By the time I'm fit enough to come back no one will even need me.' Her voice was beginning to wobble, but she carried on dejectedly, 'In two or three weeks' time, when my plaster is off, my mum will take me home to Ruislip and the hospital there will take over my care. Kate wants my flat, so everything's been taken care of.'

'Jean is getting overtired,' Claire cut in at that point. She included Lucas in her tactful reproof, but her glance was directed at Kate, who said she must be off.

Saying goodbye to Jean took no time at all, but getting out of the ward did. Kate felt she couldn't very well leave without a quick word with Sandra and her boyfriend, then on the way back a patient on traction asked her to pick up her spectacles which had fallen under her bed. By the time she reached the doors it was a struggle to get through them, due to a sudden rush of visitors. Making way for some and shouldering through the rest, she ran straight into Lucas who was hovering in the corridor, on his own, without Claire, trying to flatten himself against the wall. He was near the office, and through its half-open door Kate could see two mugs of tea, two packets of sandwiches and over the back of a chair hung a man's jacket—Lucas's jacket. It was a domestic little tableau, but without its players as yet.

'Not gone yet, I see.' Lucas managed to reach her side.

Kate grimaced. 'I'm doing my best. Getting *in* was a piece of cake, getting out is another story!'

'Docherty does better than we do for visitors, probably because the patients are rather more up to entertaining.'

'Not so much blood and guts!'

'Exactly!' Lucas laughed. 'Anyway, how are you today?' he gave her a searching glance.

'Fine, couldn't be better!' Over his shoulder Kate could see Claire talking to a male visitor.

'*And* you've found yourself a flat,' Lucas was saying. 'Now, that's what I call seizing the moment, not letting a good chance slip.'

Not particularly liking the way he'd said that, Kate put him straight. 'I don't know about that. Jean *offered* me the flat. There's no question of jumping in!'

He smiled faintly. 'Where is it?' he asked.

'Over the greengrocer's shop in Bridge Street.'

'Handy.' He looked impressed. 'Only walking distance from here. I pass those shops on my way home. I'm on the other side of the bridge, going up towards Coe Fen.'

'Really?' Kate schooled her face to look unimpressed, but had no chance to say any more for Claire appeared, bustling importantly out of the ward. 'Still here, Nurse Maybury?' She half turned to the office.

'Unfortunately, yes,' Kate replied just as pointedly, wishing both her and Lucas goodnight, leaving them to their repast in the office.

She hadn't very much liked him assuming that she'd pushed for Jean's flat, especially as, on thinking it over, she didn't know if she wanted to go ahead with it or not. Was it really worth all the hassle just for three months? It would never be *her* flat, would it? She would simply be borrowing Jean's. Jean might want the earth in rent for it and she, Kate, might not like it. All these thoughts kept her awake for most of the night.

It was a different story next day, however, for she *did* like the flat. She liked the two big rooms, the tiny kitchen and shower-room, the glimpse of the river as she gazed down the street. She liked Lew, too, a wiry little cockney with the gift of the gab. 'Pleased to meet you.' His handshake was the pumping up and down sort. 'I thought Nurse Bailey would let the flat and I like someone over me top. You fix everything up with her and give her these grapes.' He put a bunch in a paper bag. 'Give her my best and tell her I'm right sorry she's hurt her leg!'

Kate had walked back to the hospital, her head buzzing with plans which, over the next ten days, were all carried out. She found she could afford, *just* afford, the rent Jean asked. All Jean's personal things were moved out of the flat and Kate's were moved in, so the place began to look more homely and her own. Best of all, her mother raised no objection to the move. She'd almost expected it, she said, hearing Kate's promise to come home on days off with a degree of doubt, if not scepticism. Seftonbridge had more to offer socially than Cletford, even counting the interest and lure of the riding stables.

It seemed strange, that first Monday morning, waking up in the flat and walking along to the hospital in the fitful November sunshine. Once on the ward, however, and taking the hand-over report from Chloe, the usual hectic operating-day procedures blotted out everything else.

The first patient she prepped for gall-bladder removal was a thirty-year old woman called Rosa Farne who was very talkative, probably due to nerves. 'I saw Mr Brown in Outpatients,' she confided to Kate. 'When he said I had gallstones I couldn't believe it—I mean, at my age—but the scan confirmed it, so here I am for the chop!'

'With keyhole surgery it's not much of a chop,' Kate informed her. 'You'll have three tiny cuts where the instruments are inserted and the gall bladder containing the stones will be drawn out through your umbilicus. When you come to you'll have four little plasters adorning your stomach. They'll be waterproof, too, so you'll be able to bath after a day or two.'

'Doesn't sound too bad.' Rosa was sounding slurred. The premed was taking effect so, warning her not to try to get out of bed, Kate left her to rest till the porters came to collect her.

Chloe Rooke was concerned about the thyroidectomy patient with a husky throat, now on her fourth post-operative day. 'I don't think it's anything more than her larynx and trachea having been disturbed during surgery. Even so, I'd like Lucas to see her when he comes up from Theatre around teatime.'

When he came up, smelling faintly of soap and with his hair still damp from the shower, it was Kate who accompanied him into the ward, armed with Miss Law's notes and charts.

'Bit husky, are you, Miss Law?' he said, examining her throat and being careful not to ask her to bend her head back.

'Can't cough to clear it, too painful,' she rasped.

'I'm sure. Please, don't try.' He straightened, then sat on the edge of the bed. 'Now, there's nothing going wrong, nothing amiss, simply the result of surgery. What we'll try you with is an inhalant—a good old-fashioned remedy for a husky throat.'

'Will that do the trick?' She tried to perk up.

'I'd lay odds on it.' He smiled at her. 'And you're doing brilliantly, you know. Nurse here tells me that you've swallowed solid food this lunchtime without too much discomfort, and as you were what we call non-toxic at the time of surgery, there's no reason why you shouldn't sit out of bed tomorrow.'

At the ward desk Lucas updated the patient's notes, then asked Kate how the flat was.

'I only moved in last night, so I've hardly had time to realise I'm actually there. I liked being able to walk here this morning. It's a bonus, the flat being so near.'

'As you're so keen on walking, it must be!' he said with a half-grin, instantly flicking her mind back to a fortnight previously when he'd walked her back to her car from Bellini's and kissed her goodnight. She felt the colour flooding into her cheeks, but didn't think he'd noticed as Chloe appeared and he went off to meet her, calling out 'Thanks' over his shoulder, scarcely moving his head.

She saw him again, though, half an hour later when off duty and making her way along Princes Parade. He slowed his car alongside her, asking if she'd like a lift. In the welter of traffic at that time of evening, she could hardly hesitate, so with a quick dive she was in and they were drawing away from the kerb. She fastened her seat belt. 'You've got your proper car back,' she exclaimed.

'Yes, and about time, too.'

'I couldn't see how it was looking.'

'Good as new.' He was making the righthand turn into Bridge Street. 'I'm calling at Lew's,' he said. 'Need some fruit and tomatoes. That particular parade of shops serves as my local one, you know.'

'Do you cook for yourself?' she asked, surprised.

'Simple dishes, like scrambled eggs, yes,' he acknowledged with a grin. 'Mostly, though, I eat out, but, like all the food pundits advise us these days, I snack on lots of fruit.'

'Very commendable.' Kate laughed.

'I also,' he went on, 'have a visiting friend who occasionally cooks me a meal.'

'Sounds all right to me.' Kate wondered if it was Claire who did the visiting. She looked the sort who could cook.

'Well, here we are.' Lucas was drawing up outside Lew's. The lights from his and the other half-dozen shops spilled out onto the pavement. There was a fair bit of traffic passing, and Lucas called out a warning

to Kate. 'Wait, I'll come round and let you out.'
Freeing her seat belt, she stayed where she was until a
line of students had cycled past, *en route* for the bridge.
Three cars followed and it was a full minute before
Lucas appeared at her door, opened it halfway and vir-
tually pulled her out.

'You needn't have worried,' she told him on the
pavement, retrieving her arm. 'I wouldn't, for one moment, have put your brand-new door in jeopardy
again!'

'It was the other door that was damaged, and my
concern wasn't solely for the car!' he shouted close to
her ear, as a motorbike roared by.

Lew opened his shop door, saying good evening to
them both. It was Lucas who claimed most of his attention, though, and Kate scarcely had time to call out
goodnight before he was ushered into the shop like
visiting royalty.

A few minutes later, standing at the window of the
flat, she saw Lucas's car move off, its roof partly ob-
scuring Lucas from view. She kept on watching, turning sideways to the window, till the car swooped over
the bridge, then turned left towards Coe Fen and the
block of flats where he lived.

She stood there for several minutes, lost in thought.
The street was becoming more crowded with pedestri-
ans, many of them office workers on their way home.
One of them—a fair man with a briefcase—reminded
her of Clive, with whom she had lived for six months
and fancied herself in love. Clive, who was clever and
a junior partner with a firm of accountants in London.
It wasn't him, of course, but in the half-light the re-
semblance was strong. Clive had had the same spruced

neatness. She'd been crazy about him once, but he'd been difficult to live up to—a very careful man.

There were couples going by now, all hurrying home or to a pub or café, glad that their day's work was done. On the other side of the river Lucas would be putting the car away in his garage and carrying his tomatoes and fruit into the flat, where Claire would very likely join him. Bringing a bottle of wine, perhaps.

Blocking out further imaginings at this point, Kate moved from the window, trying to decide what to have for her own meal. She felt unable to settle, however, and the six o'clock news on her television did little to cheer her up. There was no doubt about it, she thought, she'd have to get organised. There was little point in living here if she didn't get out and about.

Jean, whom she visited on Thursday evening, was a mine of information when it came to things to do around the town. 'Things will have changed since your student days,' she remarked, looking gloomily down at her leg. Her plaster had been bi-valved, split from back to front, so that her knee and shin were visible, although she still had to keep the back half of the plaster in place for support. In a fortnight's time, after graduated physio, she was going home to Ruislip, where she would have continued treatment until she was fit to return to work. 'There's a new leisure centre out at Coe Fen,' she told Kate, 'with a superb skating rink. There's also the ski slope at Bartons End.' At this Kate laughed, declaring that she'd better steer clear of the latter, but that she liked the sound of the skating rink.

'Lucas and Claire both go to the leisure centre, mainly to skate so I'm told, but she works out at the gym as well to keep her curves under control,' Jean said importantly, as though she was well in the know.

'She's very pretty,' Kate replied.

'Yeah, but you're prettier. I'd give anything for a pair of legs like yours, both of them in good nick, too,' Jean sighed, then brightened up as Peter Graves, whom she quite fancied, made his way to her bed.

Kate was in the office next morning when Lucas came in to expound on a peptic ulcer patient who was being admitted at the weekend. 'She's on my list for a vagotomy on Monday. I've been seeing her in clinic.' Crossing the small room in two strides, he perched on the edge of the desk, going on to say that Mrs Arley wouldn't be an easy patient to nurse. 'She's disabled—deaf *and* blind.' He ignored Chloe's gasp. 'She was injured in a chemical factory explosion ten years ago. She's divorced and lives with her sister who communicates with her by using special touching-on-hand signals. Her sister interpreted for me all the time in clinic, so there was no real problem, but here on the ward it will be a different matter. We'll just have to get by with hand squeezes and pats of encouragement.'

'That,' Chloe said heavily, 'is all I need!'

Kate drew a deep breath, for some reason feeling acutely nervous as she blurted out in a rush, 'I have a grandfather who's deaf and blind from the Second World War. He visits us quite often and both my mother and I are used to communicating with him, using the hand technique. I learned it when I was quite young.' She paused, looking at Chloe, 'I'm fairly *au fait* with it.'

'Now, that is something!' Lucas's voice rang with surprise. Kate felt him staring at her, whilst Chloe brought her hands together with enough force to burst a bag. 'We are saved, Mr Brown!'

'Agreed. We are.' Lucas sounded relieved. 'Even so, Kate can't be on duty all the time.'

'I know that,' Chloe said practically, 'but she'll be available for morning rounds, and Mrs Arley's sister is bound to be here most afternoons, or evenings, or both, which will cover most of the ground.'

'Far better than we thought, certainly,' Lucas didn't sound too convinced, and as Kate was leaving the office to see June Tredgold, who was being discharged, she caught him looking at her in a reflective manner, as though he was wondering what other surprises she was keeping under wraps.

CHAPTER FIVE

KATE went home for the weekend, driving to Cletford on Friday evening after her late shift. It had only been six days since she'd seen her mother, but they had plenty to talk about, Paula being anxious to hear how her daughter was faring on her own.

'It feels odd,' Kate admitted, 'but, then, it's the first time I've lived on my own—ever. It feels weirdest at night, but I'm sure I'll get used to it. It'll be better when I get a social life, join some clubs and things.'

'It won't do you any harm to stand on your own feet,' Paula remarked with unmotherly brusqueness, successfully hiding the stab of anxiety she felt. 'Are you riding tomorrow?' she asked, helping herself to one of the tuna sandwiches she'd prepared for Kate.

'I thought Sunday, actually.' Kate stretched out her legs to the fire. 'I'll do the shopping tomorrow, if you like, then just flop in the afternoon.'

'Good idea.' Paula thought Kate looked tired, but refrained from saying so. 'But you'd better ring the stables first thing if you want to book Cascade.'

'Will do.' Kate abandoned her sandwiches for an apple. 'Oh, to have a horse of my own like Lucas.'

'Dream on!' Her mother laughed. 'But talking of the Browns, Lucas is home this weekend—his father told me that this morning over coffee. You won't find him at the stables, though. He's going down to Aldeburgh-on-Sea with his father. Gervase has a brother there.'

'Better and better,' Kate said stoutly, feeling a mixture of relief and disappointment, and trying not to show either. She was certainly disappointed, though, when on ringing Ann Vernon next morning, she was told that Cascade was fully booked on Sunday.

'I promised my niece she could have her, Kate, and I can't go back on my word.' Ann sounded regretful, and Kate quickly said it was her own fault for not ringing from Seftonbridge during the week.

'Raj is free, though,' Ann put in, at least during the morning. 'You've ridden him before, haven't you? He'd be thrilled out of his bit to have you on his back again!'

Kate laughed. She liked Ann, greatly admiring the way she and her husband ran the stables. They really loved their horses and their care of them was second to none. Had that not been the case, Lucas would never have left Hercules with them, she was sure. 'I'd love to ride Raj again,' she said, and the booking was made.

Sunday dawned, not bright and fair but dull and threatening rain. Still, there hadn't been rain for ages, so the ground would be all right, Kate was thinking as she got into her riding gear, zipping up her jodhpurs, dragging a thick-knit sweater over her head. The bottle green of the sweater suited her tawny hair which she'd pulled back in a single plait.

Setting off for the stables shortly after ten o'clock, she felt the usual excited anticipation, and couldn't get there fast enough. Even so, she wasn't the first to arrive, for as she entered the yard four horses and riders were already setting off. Sunday morning was a popular riding time. She realised then that she wished Lucas was amongst them, that she would see him on the heath. Then, on her way to the tack room to fetch her hard hat, she *did* see him.

For a moment she blinked, unable to believe that it really was him, fully mounted, about to move out of the yard. He wasn't looking her way and she didn't make the mistake of calling out to him. Hercules's reaction to a sudden call might make him nervous. Not only that but Lucas himself might not be pleased to see her. When all was said and done, she didn't really know him all that well, she reminded herself, standing out of range as horse and rider moved out of the yard. Watching them go, she wondered what had happened to the Aldeburgh trip her mother had told her about.

A few minutes later, astride Raj, she entered Loamers Lane. A fine drizzle was falling, clotting her lashes, making vision difficult. Not that this mattered too much for Raj knew the territory. Glad to be out with a light load on his back, he was longing to be off and away. Once out on the open heath Kate allowed him to canter, adjusting her hips to the rocking movement, enjoying it as much as he, both of them revelling in the cold gush of air as they cleaved their way through it. Kate even forgot Lucas. She forgot everything but the thrill of being astride a powerful horse and cantering over Cletford Heath.

But her happiness was to be short-lived. Nothing prepared her for imminent disaster. She had no warning at all before a flash of red-brown streaked in from the side in front of Raj's hooves. She just had time to register it was a fox before the stallion screamed and reared and she was sliding off his back, nerveless hands losing the reins, feet slipping out of the stirrups. There was a glimpse of sky, a great wall of horse, and then she was flat on her back, winded, half-stunned, listening to Raj galloping off.

She was too winded, too jolted, too scared to move,

but when at last she did, Raj was a fleeing streak in the distance, making for Fenton Wood. She coughed and gasped and eased herself up. She *had* to catch him. To return to the stables without him was too awful to contemplate, not that she could contemplate much at all, but she *must* get him back.

She moved cautiously, inch by inch, and eventually stood up. Nothing gave way so she was still in one piece. And now she had to find Raj. She headed for the wood, hoping that he'd have slowed down amongst the trees. But supposing he'd injured himself in there, broken his neck in terror? She felt sick at the thought of it. Most riders walked their horses through the wood. But then again someone might have found him and calmed him down. Praying out loud, Kate started half walking, half running, reeling about like a drunk.

Inside the wood the narrow paths were indented with hoofprints. It was always like that, summer or winter, no grass had the chance to grow. Was Raj here? She started to give the call that Ann always used for her horses. She called until she was hoarse.

Then, just as she was starting to panic, she heard the sound of a horse—no, horses—approaching at walking pace. Some riders were coming this way. They must have seen Raj, seen which way he'd gone. As the trees thinned she saw them—two horses and a man—Raj and Hercules, Lucas between them, holding the reins of both.

'Oh, thank goodness! Oh, Lucas, you've got him!' She almost fell to her knees with relief and weakness and thankfulness, seeing in a blur the dishevelled figure in front of her, his hair blown and awry, looking amazed, even shocked at the sight of her.

'Kate, what on earth…?' His voice was a bellow,

and she realised that he equated her with Cascade. To him Cascade was *her* horse, Raj was not, so, on finding him loose, the fact that she might have been his rider hadn't occurred to him.

Feeling too shaky to explain, she leaned against a tree, drawing in great gulps of air, for to pass out as well as lose her seat would have been too ignominious.

Lucas, his back turned, was tethering the horses, then he came back to her, unbuckling her hat, lifting it off, letting it drop to the ground. She should sit down, he knew that, but the ground was too wet. His eyes raked her length, looking, she supposed, for spikes of bone sticking out through her clothes. She shivered and he gripped her shoulders.

'Are you hurt?' His voice was sharp but pulled her together and focussed her attention.

'No, I'm not,' she told him steadily, then managed a grin. 'And we've had this conversation before.'

'When? What do you mean?'

'In the tack room, when I slipped up on the soap you left lying around!'

'Oh, right, yes.' He didn't smile back. He was virtually holding her up, with the help of the tree at her back. 'But what exactly happened, and why weren't you riding Cascade?'

'A fox streaked out in front of us, Raj bucked and reared and I lost the reins and slid down his back. He went off like a bat out of hell. Cascade was booked so I couldn't have her. She's out on the heath some-where!' Kate was babbling, and knew she was, but she was so conscious of Lucas, so aware of him, that her breath kept catching in little jerks. She tried to look at the horses across the path, but his shoulder was in the way and had little bits of twig on it. She itched to brush

them off. Kate shifted slightly, away from the tree
which was cutting into her back, and his hands fell
from her shoulders. It was then that she saw the blood
on his cheek, which seemed to be coming from a
wound higher up.

'It's you who is hurt. You're bleeding!' She turned
his face to one side. 'You've got a graze or cut just
above your eyebrow!' Gently she touched the spot.

'Damn!' It didn't seem to pain him and he let her
investigate. 'I thought I came up against something
when I leaned over from the saddle to make a grab for
Raj. He didn't just stand there all docile, waiting to be
caught!' Lucas glowered at Kate as though it had been
her fault, which in a sense it had been.

'Oh, I'm sorry!' She felt in her pocket for a tissue.

'That's when I lost my hat!'

'Pity!' Refraining from saying sorry again, she asked
him to keep still. 'And don't touch it.' She brushed his
hand down. 'Let me clean you up a bit. What you need
is a plaster.' She put the bloodied tissue that she'd used
to wipe his face back into her pocket.

'I may be a doctor, but it's not a thing I normally
carry around.'

'No, I suppose not.'

'I'm on my way to visit friends at Betchworth.'

'Then ask them for one,' she said. 'Most people keep
plasters tucked away in their kitchen drawers.'

'Do they?' he answered, without even listening to
her. His face was still close.

'Yes.' She didn't move back, her hand was still on
his shoulder and their eyes met at close range, his full
of desire, intent, flickering over her face. 'Lucas!' she
swallowed convulsively.

'Kate.' There was a harsh-breathing pause, then he

snatched her close, fastening his mouth over hers. Passion roared in like a flood-tide, engulfing them both, and she let it take her, gave herself up to it. Nothing mattered but this.

When he loosened her she was sure she was dying. 'We have company,' he whispered, as a string of riders passed at close range, one remarking on the worsening rain, which was dripping down through the trees.

Kate bent to pick up her hat, fitting it on with shaking hands. 'That was close!' She was straining to laugh.

'It was, and we'd better get on.' Lucas was turning away to untether the horses, seeming to take a long time. When he came back, walking between them, he looked grim but purposeful, 'Kate.' He looked straight at her. 'I'm sure you feel as I do, that it would be better if we didn't become emotionally involved. What happened just now was delightful, but—'

'Say no more!' she broke in, forcing her stiff face to smile. 'I feel exactly as you do, but don't look so worried, it was only a kiss after all!'

His throat moved as he swallowed. 'I wouldn't like you to think—'

'I'm not thinking anything right now, I'm too wet and cold.' Taking Raj from him and preparing to mount, she heard him ask if she was fit to ride after her fall.

'Of course, but I'll turn back, I think. I don't want to ride on in this rain.' She put her foot in the stirrup he was holding steady for her, carefully avoiding his gaze, but once in the saddle and looking down at him she was consumed with longing again. It was all she could do to stay mounted and not slide down into his arms.

'I'll ride back with you.' He flung his leg over

Hercules's back, walking him a little ahead, calling back to her, 'You had a nasty fall, you should never have been allowed out on Raj.'

'Rubbish! I often have Raj, and I'm OK, really. You've got to get to Betchworth and I'll be fine on my own. I don't like riding in tandem anyway.' This was another thrust home.

'OK, if you're sure.' He didn't look round, 'I have to admit that I don't want to be later than I am already.' He was several yards ahead, flinging words over his shoulder—blaming words, no doubt. The path was narrow, too narrow for two horses to walk side by side. Even so, trailing along in his wake like some kind of follow my leader caused a smarting resentment to build up in Kate, making her want to throw something or shout out something rude.

Once through the wood and on the open heath, they prepared to part, Lucas turning Hercules in a wide arc to face Betchworth and the villages beyond.

'Take care.' He was watching her pull the brim of her hat well down. She nodded without speaking, nudging Raj forward, and then they were off, riding away in opposite directions like characters in a film.

Kate cantered bumpily back to the stables, co-ordinating badly, her cheeks burning despite the cold rain which was driving into her. The heat came from anger. She was angry with herself, angry because she knew she had invited Lucas to kiss her, standing up close to him, dabbing at his face for far longer than she'd needed, with her arm halfway round his neck. She had opened herself to him, shown herself to him, shown him what she was feeling, and he'd responded, too, but had regretted it afterwards. He'd already got a girlfriend and she, Kate, had known that. Whatever had she been thinking about? And now she was wet and miserable. Tears rolled down her face, and she licked at their dripping saltiness as she entered Loamers Lane.

Because she had never seen Claire out of uniform and had never thought to see her in Cletford, she didn't at first recognise the small figure in a waxed jacket getting out of a yellow sports car at the entrance to the stableyard. It wasn't until she came running across and was near enough for Kate to look straight down at her that recognition struck like a bolt of lightning. Oh, dear God, not *her*!

Claire was the first to speak. 'Fancy meeting you here!' she exclaimed.

'I could say the same about you.' Kate slid down from the saddle, shortening Raj's reins, trying to keep his head still. 'I ride out from here,' she told Claire. 'My home's just over there.'

'I didn't know that.' Claire's pretty face blanked, then, recovering, she said, 'Lucas keeps a horse here—you probably know that—and it's him I've come about. He's supposed to be at my home now, at Betchworth, but hasn't turned up. I tried his mobile, but he's got it switched off. Have you seen him, by any chance?'

'Yes, I have,' Kate volunteered carefully. 'We met on the heath. He helped me catch Raj.' She put a hand on the stallion's neck. 'I fell off him, you see, and he bolted, but Lucas caught up with him. He said he was on his way to Betchworth. I'm just sorry I made him late.'

'So he's on his way now?'

'Yes, he is.'

'And how long ago was this?'

'I would think about fifteen minutes.'

'In that case, he should be there by now...' Claire

looked at her watch '...being entertained by my father who wants to see his horse, which is why, on this piddling morning, he's travelling on hoof!'

'Actually, the rain wasn't so heavy earlier on.' Kate felt she had to point out, just as a movement inside Claire's parked car caught her attention. Its door was opening and a fair-haired man of lanky build was ejecting himself onto the cobbles.

'Any luck?' he called out, arranging a newspaper over his head.

'Yes, he's on his way. Get back in, Hugh, no sense in us both getting wet! That's my cousin, by the way, just home from abroad,' Claire told Kate, her smile flashing out as she ran off to the car.

She reversed, turned and shot down the drive, leaving a very shaken Kate to lead Raj across the yard. Claire was the last person she'd wanted to see—the absolute last. No one could have made her feel worse.

She turned down Iris's offer to unsaddle Raj for her. 'I'll do it,' she said. 'I'd like to, I'm the reason why he's in such a mess!'

The fact was that she didn't want to go home yet. She wanted, needed the close company of the horse, the physical effort it took to tend him in his loose box. Its warm, dry, straw-smelling interior soothed her as it did him, the movements of her arms as she wiped and brushed him, slicking off wet and mud, calmed her like nothing else. She talked to him as she worked.

It wasn't until she was going along to the tack room, his saddle over her arm, that reality kicked in again, forcing her to think of Lucas with Claire and her family, perhaps having a drink before lunch. Claire would have attended to that graze on his head and been told how it had happened. She would have told him how surprised she had been to run into Kate at the stables.

She applied herself vigorously to the task of cleaning Raj's tackle, washing the snaffle under the running tap, splashing her boots and legs. Well, at least, she thought, Claire's surprise seems to indicate that he doesn't tell her everything. Perhaps she's the sort to make something out of nothing, and he likes to keep the peace. For some reason this made her feel very nearly in league with him.

CHAPTER SIX

'WE'VE put her in bed six just inside the doors,' Chloe told Kate on Monday. She was referring to the deaf and blind patient, Mrs Arley, whom Kate could see through the viewing window, knitting something pink as though her life depended on it. 'She's nervous, that's obvious. Go and talk to her, Kate, and start prepping her in about half an hour. Mr Brown wants her in Theatre by half-ten. These are her notes. He's going to operate through the thorax, so she'll be on underwater seal drainage when she comes out of Theatre. I'm sure he's explained all that to her, via her sister, but it might help her if you go over it with her. I want her to get used to you.'

That I should be so popular, Kate was thinking as she went towards Irene's bed. She deliberately sat on the edge of it, knowing that the slight movement of the mattress would alert her to the fact that someone was near. Irene was fifty-two, still dark-haired. One side of her face had had plastic surgery, so well done that she was pretty rather than just presentable, and her slightly crooked smile showed strong white teeth. She was smiling now, waiting to be 'spoken' to.

Gently Kate took her left hand and turned it palm up. Instantly, even before she had started to communicate, Irene said in a loud, slightly thickened voice, 'Oh, you're able to talk to me. Who are you? Are you a lady doctor?'

'Not a doctor. I'm a nurse,' Kate signed on her hand.

'But I am one of the people who will be looking after you.'

'You can sign!' There was no mistaking the relief in Irene's voice and on her face.

After a few more signed words on the palm of Irene's hand, letting her know that she would soon be prepped for surgery and what to expect afterwards, Kate crossed the ward to introduce herself to two other new admissions—the first a Mrs Royle, with a lump in her breast, the second a lady in her seventies for a haemorroidectomy. Both were curious about Irene Arley.

'Can't she hear at all?' Mrs Royle asked.

'No, I'm afraid not. She can't see either,' Kate replied, not wanting to chat about Irene unduly but feeling that some explanation was due.

'But she's not deaf and dumb?' Mrs Harding in the next bed asked.

'No, she can talk.'

'It's lucky you can do that sign stuff on her hand.' Mrs Harding's own voice altered at that point, and she put her spectacles on in a kind of flurried excitement.

Turning to see what had caught her attention, Kate saw Lucas entering the ward. He went straight to the nurses' station, crooking a beckoning finger at her.

'He wants you, love,' Mrs Harding sighed enviously as Kate sped off to attend to him, disciplining her thoughts, acting for all she was worth.

He greeted her smilingly but totally impersonally, and she was grateful for that. She took her cue from him, not even mentioning the little strip of plaster above his right eyebrow. 'I've very little time.' He looked at the big clock over the doors. 'But I'd like you to introduce me to Mrs Arley, see if she remembers me from the outpatients clinic.'

'I'm sure she will. She strikes me as being right on the ball, very quick to cotton on. She's learned Braille, which makes a great difference when writing on her hand as she picks up the shortened version of the words and I noticed, just now, that I often didn't need to finish sentences.'

By this time they were at Irene's bedside, and Kate was taking her hand and signing on it, 'It's Kate again, Irene.'

'Oh, I knew who it was,' she replied, and Kate wondered how, then remembered that she was the only one around who could communicate with her. 'I've brought Mr Lucas Brown, your surgeon, to see you,' she continued. 'He's the one who—'

'I saw in Outpatients,' Irene finished, putting out her right hand, which was warmly shaken by Lucas.

'Tell her,' Lucas proceeded to tell Kate, 'that I'm pleased to have her under my care, that she has nothing to worry about and that once the discomfort of the first few post-op days are over she'll be feeling much better and have a good quality of life in front of her.'

Kate's flying fingers made swift work of all this and it amused her to think that if she'd wanted to add something rude about Lucas there was nothing to stop her. He would never ever know unless Irene gave her away. 'Tell her she's in safe hands,' he was concluding, and Kate fully conveyed this, adding, 'The safest ever. Mr Brown is the bee's knees.'

Smiling and laughing, Irene said, 'Thank you.'

'What did you say to her?' Lucas asked Kate suspiciously as they walked towards the doors.

His glance at her was searching and, recognising

possible danger signs, Kate quickly replied, 'I added that you were good. I expect Mrs Arley just laughed in relief, you know how it is.'

'Everything all right?' Chloe popped out of her office. She had watched Kate's performance through the viewing window with considerable admiration. 'I think,' she said, looking at Lucas, 'that the sooner you and I learn this method of communication the better, Mr Brown, otherwise, unbeknown to us, Nurse Maybury and Mrs Arley will be having jokes at our expense.'

Kate could feel herself colouring.

Lucas noticed and said, 'You echo my thoughts exactly, Sister.' He smiled stiffly as he swept up the corridor, muttering about being late.

Kate not only prepped Irene for surgery, but accompanied her down to the theatre suite, staying with her and holding her hand whilst she was given the anaesthetic. All unconscious patients were vulnerable, but somehow or other Irene seemed more so, extra lonely and lost. Watching her being taken into the theatre, watching its doors open and close, Kate was conscious of a rock-like lump in her throat as she turned to go back to her ward. Once there, however, other patients claimed her thoughts. Mrs Royle, for instance, needed to be told that her lump might not necessitate losing the whole of her breast. 'You may just need to have what we call a lumpectomy which simply leaves a scar.' It wasn't up to her to say more than this. Either the consultant, Mr Chance, or Lucas would have said most of it anyway. All the woman wanted was repeated reassurance. As I would, if it were me, Kate thought, injecting the premed drug into Mrs Royle's left buttock and leaving her to rest.

Mrs Harding, in the next bed, appeared to have no qualms about her haemorrhoidectomy. 'I've been waiting long enough, and I'm glad to be here at last. Haemorrhoids aren't nice things to have, dear. I tell my husband that when I'm good and rid of them, we'll go out and celebrate.'

She was the last patient Kate prepped before midday. Chloe, supervising the patients' lunches, told her to go off duty at twelve-thirty and not come on again till half past four. 'I want you to be here when Mrs Arley surfaces,' she said. 'The sister won't be coming in until tomorrow, I've advised her not to, but the poor woman will need someone with her who can *indicate* how she is.'

Even though that would mean a long evening shift, Kate agreed at once. She wasn't doing anything special anyway, and as Chloe would be going off at half past four it meant that once more she would be in charge. Kate was beginning to relish responsibility now that she was accustomed to the ward, and she was proud of being able to help Irene Arley, not to mention four other newly post-operative patients who would be back from Theatre by late afternoon.

It was good to feel wanted, good to feel relied on, and her step was light when a few minutes later she stepped out into the thin November sunshine, well wrapped up against the cold. Her tightly belted navy coat suited her willowy shape, her shiny hair in its bulbous bun suited the coat. She strode up Bridge Street *en route* for Lew's, and the flat, and scrambled eggs on toast. Then she changed her mind, and walked on. She would treat herself to lunch out. It would cost her a bomb, but would be worth it. A working girl needed her viands. So she whisked past the shop, wav-

ing to Lew, who was dragging in a crate of sprouts.
She knew where she was going—to the River Lawns
Hotel, owned and run by the Chancellors, who were
friends of her mother's. Their daughter, Anna—now
married with children—had been the orthopaedic sister
at the General before Claire Jevons had arrived.

It wasn't far to the hotel—just a little to the left from
Bridge Street on the same side of the river. It stood in
lush green lawns well back from the towpath. It was a
popular meeting place for businessmen and -women,
and dons and students alike.

And its dining room was full, Kate saw as she
walked across the foyer, glancing through the glass
double doors. Then, as she'd hoped she would, she
caught the eye of Lois Chancellor, who was talking to
a waiter. She came out and greeted Kate enthusiasti-
cally, asked about her mother then, hearing she was
hoping to eat in the restaurant, darted back to the
waiter—she was the quick-moving type—and got him
to set up a table for one just inside the doors. 'It's not
the best seat in the house, Kate, but the food will make
up for that. Now, come and have a drink with me whilst
it's being prepared,' she suggested, so off they went to
the bar.

Kate's table by the doors, some twenty minutes later,
afforded her a view of most of the people in the long
dining room. Her eye passed idly over them as she ate
her fish. Most were business people, she thought, although there were several tourists, easily picked out by
their packs and tote bags stowed under their tables. It
wasn't until she moved her chair slightly to avoid being
bumped by incomers that she spotted two men by the
riverside windows, talking earnestly together. One, the
elder one, was facing her. The other showed only his

back, but it was a back view Kate knew and recognised instantly—the sleek hair, fair to sandy, the set of his shoulders. It was Clive. Good lord, it was *Clive*. What on earth was he doing here?

She carried on eating and looking, gulping at her water glass and feeling disturbed as well as shocked. The last time she had seen him had been six months ago when he'd come to her home, to Cruse Cottage at Cletford, while she'd been convalescing after being mugged—a kind of watershed time.

Perhaps he was here on business; perhaps the man with him was one of the partners in his company. They were at the coffee stage of their meal, and would probably be leaving in a minute. Clive would see her for sure, she was more or less a sitting target right here by the doors.

She finished her fish, refused a second course, ordered coffee and waited, still feeling dry-mouthed and tense for it was impossible not to feel *something* for the man who had been her first lover. He would certainly be surprised when he saw her, for he'd have had no warning. At least she'd had time to gather her wits whilst staring at his head and shoulders for the last few minutes.

The waiter had poured her first cup of coffee and left her to drink it when Clive and his companion rose from their table and began their walk to the doors. Clive spotted her at once. She saw his head jerk up, saw him hesitate for a second and then he came swiftly forward to stand in front of her, leaving his companion ambling behind.

'Kate, I can hardly believe it!' He looked flushed and a little thrown.

'Hello, Clive. Good to see you.' The more composed

of the two, Kate was able to smile at him perfectly naturally.

Meantime Clive's companion had joined them and was introduced to her as Clive's senior partner, Marcus Brandt. 'Marcus, this is Kate Maybury, an old…a very dear friend, who lives out at Cletford,' Clive supplied.

'Does she now?' Marcus Brandt's solid warm hand wrapped itself round Kate's. 'Well, now I know why Clive was so keen to come on this audit,' he said, his small, dark, twinkly eyes boring into Kate's.

'So you're here on business.' With her hand back again, Kate looked from him to Clive.

But before he could answer, Marcus, plainly not lacking in tact, muttered something about needing to leave. 'You stay, Clive, I'll see you back at Barchesters in half an hour. And I hope to see you again some time, Miss Maybury.' With that he made his exit, shouldering his way through a crowd of undergraduates piling in through the doors.

A little awkwardness settled on Kate and Clive, neither knowing quite what to say or how to begin, and when they *did* begin they both spoke at once and laughed self-consciously.

'It's a little late in the day to be shy of one another,' Kate said, and they laughed again, Clive suggesting that they should go somewhere more private to talk. Kate agreed, not surprised at the request as the poor man was having to bend double to speak to her, as well as being bumped by the doors. 'I'll just pay my bill, then we can leave,' she said. 'We can walk along the towpath for a bit, it's not raining or anything, and we can keep an eye on the time.'

Clive fell in with this plan only too readily, and a few minutes later saw them on the towpath, making for the bridge. It was windy and chilly, and Clive had no coat. 'I seldom wear a topcoat, I don't feel the cold,' he reminded her, as they stood at the centre point of the bridge, looking down at the greenish translucent water flowing downstream to the lock.

'I'd forgotten,' she said, then felt she'd been tactless, for it hadn't been all that long ago since Clive and she had been a couple. He had always been a keep-fit enthusiast, jogging and working out at one of the gyms in South London. He'd even run the London Marathon. Quite often, in comparison, she'd felt positively slothful for not measuring up.

'You're looking well, Kate, very smart, too.' He turned round to face her, his hazel eyes under thick sandy brows taking in her long trim shape in her navy coat, the glowing tinge to her skin.

'Where are you nursing—here, in Seftonbridge?'

'Yes, at the General,' she said, 'through an agency. I'm on the surgical unit, taking the place of someone who's off sick.'

'Agency nursing—that's a new one for you!'

'Lots of things are new,' she said, sensing faint criticism, although, of course, she could be wrong. 'How long are you here for?' she asked, trying to keep the conversation going.

'Three or four weeks.'

'That's a long audit!'

'Actually, it's two,' he replied. 'We're at Barchesters first, then move on to Retford Chemicals on the Seftonbridge-Cletford Road. Marcus is staying at the hotel. I've got digs in Elvington Road, just across the river.'

'Are they all right?' Clive was fussy, he wouldn't put up with much.

'Well, as I didn't take them up until late last night

it's a little too soon to tell. I'm the only lodger and my landlady, Mrs Boon, is a woman in her fifties or sixties, whose late husband, so she tells me, was a don at Peterhouse.'

'You were lucky,' Kate pointed out, 'to get any-where in mid-term. I've got a flat. Aren't I the lucky one?'

'Here in Seftonbridge?' He sounded surprised and clearly interested.

'Yes, in Bridge Street. The nurse whose place I've taken has gone home to convalesce. She's sub-let me her flat till the new year so, instead of driving back-wards and forwards to Cletford each day, I can soci-alise in my spare time.'

'Your mother will miss you.'

'I go home on my days off. Clive, talking of time, we've been here roughly a quarter of an hour and if you're to get to Barchesters within the half hour, you ought to be starting off now.'

'You're right.' Pushing back the sleeve of his jacket, he looked at his watch.

'I'll come part of the way with you, if you like. I'm not on shift till half-four.'

'I *would* like.' They walked back to the towpath side by side. 'It's so good to see you, Kate. I was going to ring you at Cletford, you know, thinking you were still living at home, but it was late when we got here last night and then, well, surprise, surprise, I run into you by chance!'

'I was pretty surprised to see you.' She laughed. 'I'd been admiring your back view for some time before you turned round.'

They entered Bridge Street, Clive meticulously walking on the kerb side of the pavement. 'Can we meet again?' he asked abruptly. 'Perhaps have a drink together one evening, see a film or something like that? I'm here for an awful lot of evenings, and I'd love to hear all your news.'

Kate wasn't surprised at the invitation, she had sensed it simmering right from that moment in the restaurant when he'd wanted to 'go somewhere quiet to talk'. All he'd have done if he'd *not* wanted to see her again would have been to have greeted her and then departed with Mr Brandt. So, in a way, she'd decided to accept his invitation even before he'd given it breath.

'That would be really nice,' she told him. 'I don't know many people here yet, not in Seftonbridge, I mean.' She halted, suddenly thinking of Lucas, then dismissed him from her mind, hearing Clive enthusing at her side.

'That's great!' Surprise rang in his voice.

'Surely you didn't think I'd refuse,' she teased.

'I wasn't sure. After all, you wouldn't see me in London after your convalescent period at home.'

'That was different.' She wriggled away from that one. 'We hadn't long split up,' she said.

He let that go. 'So, can we meet tonight?' He was eager now, and bolder too, slipping a hand through her arm, reacting a little when she shook her head.

'I'm on shift till just before ten, Clive. This is one of my late nights. Tomorrow, yes, I could manage that.'

'So could I, even better than this evening,' he agreed readily. He was just about to ask where they should meet when she drew him to a stop in front of Lew's, pointing upwards.

'*Voilà*, my flat, with its splendid view of the opposite side of the street!'

Clive's neatly barbered sandy head tilted to view it. 'Over a *shop*!' he exclaimed.

'It's near the hospital.' Kate rose to defend it. 'It's a greengrocer's and Lew, the proprietor, is an absolute sweetie!' She simmered a bit. Clive had snobbery running right through him, it had been one of the things that had made her explode when they'd been living together.

'I didn't mean…' he sounded contrite.

'Of course you did,' she said, waving at Lew who was bagging up potatoes in the shop. He waved back, grinning and sticking his thumbs up in the air.

'I just wondered,' Clive was saying, 'if it was secure, if you were safe.'

'As houses,' Kate riposted stoutly. 'There's a street door.' She pointed it out. 'It's locked at night. Then up the stairs is the main door of the flat which has a lock and chain!'

'In that case, sorry to be critical.' Clive took a last look up at the flat. 'It's simply that after what happened in London…'

'Please, don't mention that. I'm trying to forget it,' Kate told him, her normal good humour reasserting itself. She slipped her hand through his arm. 'Come on, or you really will be late. I need to go into the town centre, so you've got me all the way!'

'Splendid!' They smiled at one another, and Lew, glancing out at them, thought what a smashing young couple they made—posh-looking, classy, like the sort you see on the TV.

The thought came to Kate as they walked along that Clive's arrival in Seftonbridge just at this juncture was no bad thing for either of them. She needed someone to go out with and so did he, at least for the time he was working here. She might even, in his company, manage to forget having made such a fool of herself with Lucas yesterday. Clive was a friend...still a friend. Glancing at his thin, clever face, at his pointy nose with the mark on the bridge where his reading glasses sat, she felt a comforting warmth spreading over her. Lucas could go to hell.

She had been on shift nearly four hours when he poked his dark head round the office door. In no way had she expected him, not at this time of night. There had been no crisis and the newly post-op patients were still semi-comatose, surfacing briefly then sleeping again, not wanting to be disturbed.

'A late visit!' She strained to smile and look businesslike.

'True enough.' He didn't smile back, but went on to say that he was concerned about Mrs Arley.

'That's why I'm here,' Kate said, getting up from her chair. 'Sister wanted someone around who could reassure her if she needed it.' She swallowed against a dry throat.

'That's good.'

'Yes, isn't it?'

'I'd like to see her obs.' He was almost as staccato as she. He's tired to death, she thought, feeling a reluctant sympathy as they went into the ward. He glanced at the charts then at Irene, who was lying in a propped-up position, deeply asleep, a nasogastric tube in place. Another tube ran into her arm and yet another snaked its way from her chest into a bottle of water on the floor. As she inhaled, the water rose in the tube, and when exhaling the water level went down. Lucas watched it critically. 'There has never,' he commented, 'been a better way of indicating what's going on in a patient's pleural space. I'm sure you know how important it is that the tube doesn't kink?'

'I do, and I also know that the tube has to be clamped if the bottle is changed.' Kate said this agreeably enough, but he got the message at once.

'Sorry.' She felt his swift glance. 'Sometimes I forget—'

'That I'm not a first-year student let loose on the ward!' Again, she said this laughingly, and he responded at once.

'Sorry again.' She felt him touch her shoulder. 'But twelve hours in Theatre is taking its toll, I'm afraid.'

Once back in the corridor, Marcia, Zelda's stand-in, appeared from the ward kitchen, asking—with her eyes on Lucas—if they'd like some refreshment.

'A pot of tea would be very welcome.' He looked at Kate, who agreed. 'I can't stand the coffee they make on the wards,' he told her in the office.

'Perhaps you're too fussy.' Kate, with her back to him, was replacing Irene's notes in the cabinet. She was trying her hardest to school her face not to show the ridiculous, and dangerous, pleasure she was feeling at him not rushing off. Would he mention yesterday? She hoped not, then conversely hoped he would. Should she mention his head and ask how it was? Don't be silly, of course she mustn't.

When the tray was brought in there were four chocolate digestives lying on a plate next to the pot. Nothing, it seemed, was too good for the likes of Lucas Brown!

'Didn't you have any supper?' he asked her, watching her eat her share of the biscuits.

'You mean because I'm pigging?'

'Certainly not,' he denied, 'but you do have a rather lean and hungry look.'

'That's my type.' She nodded, reaching for the teapot. 'And, yes, I did have supper, but a snatched one, just sandwiches down here.'

'You should have had your proper break,' he told her sternly, noting the shadows under her eyes.

'I had a four-hour break at midday,' she informed him, 'and a hotel lunch.'

'Did you now?' He looked at her questioningly, but when she volunteered nothing else, he began to talk of Irene Arley and of Kate's skill in communicating with her. 'You're so quick and deft.'

'Comes with practice.' She looked at him carefully. Was he flattering her and, if so, why? But perhaps he was just being nice. 'She's an intelligent lady,' she went on, 'and it helps that she's vocal—a bonus that she's not mute.'

'I expect you get lots of practice with your grandfather.'

'Yes,' she said, 'I do.'

Lucas, who had been watching her face, stirred his tea carefully. 'I'd like to learn the language,' he said after a pause.

'Well, there's nothing to stop you,' she said briskly. 'There's a special manual alphabet for the deaf-blind, published by the RNIB. It contains several pages of clear illustrations. Anyone can learn from those.'

'I'll send for a copy.'

'Good idea.' Kate settled the cups back on the tray. 'The only thing is, by the time you get it, Irene will have been discharged.'

'I'll be seeing her in Outpatients for some time, and

extra skills are never wasted,' Lucas replied flatly, wishing Kate would meet his eye.

From across the corridor, through in the sluice, bowls were being filled—wash-bowls for bedridden patients who were being settled down for the night. Any minute now the night staff would arrive and, conscious of what she should be doing, Kate's glance swept past his head as she looked through the viewing window.

'I can see you want to turn me out.' He rose to his feet, blocking her view for a second. She, too, got up.

'Actually,' she said, feeling that she hadn't been overly helpful to him, 'you could borrow our pamphlet—my mother's and mine. We never need to use it, but I know there's a copy at home. Mother's coming to Seftonbridge tomorrow to treat a patient at the Leahurst Nursing Home. I could ring her tonight and ask her to drop it into the flat with some other stuff I want.'

Lucas turned slowly round from the door, 'That would be great, if it wouldn't be putting your mother to too much trouble. I'm being annoying, aren't I?' He smiled and Kate caught her breath. Why did he have to be so attractive, why did he make her feel that she would bend over backwards to help him, no matter what?

Out in the corridor she was able to say goodnight to him with her usual professional calm. At the far end, through the landing doors, the night nurses emerged, whilst Nurse Liu, emerging from the sluice, smiled at him round her tower of bedpans, nearly toppling them over his feet.

'Nice try!' He returned her smile, and as he sped up the corridor it occurred to Kate, not for the first time, that with no trouble at all he could charm any female senseless.

CHAPTER SEVEN

As IT turned out, it was Kate's mother who rang shortly after Kate got home, explaining that she wouldn't be able to meet her the next day. 'I've had to fit in another appointment after the Leahurst one,' she said, 'but I can still bring all the things you asked for and drop them at the flat. Lew knows me and he'll unlock the street door, and I've got a key to your flat.'

'I'll tell Lew you'll be coming, and thanks,' Kate said. 'There's something else. Clive's here on an audit... Yes, Clive. I ran into him today.' She waited until her mother had finished exclaiming, then went on to ask her to bring her tennis racket and skates. 'And my joggers and trainers... Yes, we're going to meet and be healthily motivated whilst Clive's here. You know what he's like, but it might be fun and it'll get me out and about.' There were more exclamations and questions to be answered before Kate could broach the subject of the deaf-blind pamphlet. 'It's for Lucas Brown.' She explained the circumstances. 'I said he could borrow ours to save him sending for one. He wants to get started at once.'

'Now, that sounds like the wish of a sensible, well-intentioned male,' Paula commented, saying that she thought she could lay her hands on the pamphlet with no trouble at all. 'Darling, I'm so sorry I won't see you tomorrow, but you'll be here at the weekend, won't you?'

After a little more along these lines, the call was

concluded, and Kate sat there with the mobile in her lap, thinking over the events of the day, getting up at last to switch on the television and watch the end of the ten o'clock news.

Ten o'clock next morning saw her with Irene again, who wanted reassurance that things were going well. 'Couldn't be better,' Kate wrote on her hand. 'In two or three days' time you may even be rid of your underwater seal tube.'

'I'm afraid to move in case I upset the jar.' Irene's tongue moved over her dry teeth. She was trying her best to smile.

'You won't. We're all keeping an eye on it. We're an efficient lot in here!' Kate jested, laying Irene's hand back on the coverlet.

Further up the ward May Boughton, the new agency nurse, was prepping the appendix case—a girl of fifteen. Donna had been admitted via Casualty that morning, accompanied by her distraught mother, who had only just gone. 'And thank heavens for that.' May frowned as Kate came to the bedside. 'She upset the girl more than calmed her, going on about her being all she had—you know the sort of thing!'

Kate did, and said so, setting her premed tray down on the locker whilst May went off to her coffee-break, a shade indignant at not being left to give the teenager the injection herself.

Hoping that Donna hadn't heard her remarks about her mother, Kate chatted to her, hoping to allay her fears. 'In no time at all now, Donna, that troublesome appendix will be taken away, and you'll be back here in the ward.'

The girl smiled, but didn't speak. She was very

flushed and kept moving her arms. People in pain were seldom still, as Kate knew only too well. Donna was compliant, though, and made no fuss when asked to roll over so that the premed drugs could be injected into her buttock. 'Just a nasty little jab. There you are, all done.' Kate pulled Donna's gown back down. 'In a minute or two you'll begin to feel woozy, and that horrible pain will feel a long way off, as though it belongs to someone else.'

'I'll be fine, don't worry,' Donna said, amazing Kate till she realised that quite likely the girl's remark was the sort she often had to make to her over-anxious mother.

Daphne Harding called her over then, wanting to know when her dressing and that 'tube thing' could be taken out.

'Mr Brown will decide that,' Kate told her, 'but probably not for another two or three days. I expect it feels uncomfortable, does it?'

'Like being stuffed!' she said with a grin that became a grimace, and Kate sympathised. Lying on one's side was a trying position, making things like looking at a paper or magazine almost impossible. 'So, when's Mr Good-Looking coming in again?' she asked, and Kate knew she meant Lucas.

'Most likely later today when he's out of Theatre.' Kate bent to retrieve a wisp of cotton wool floating about on the floor.

'Do you think he likes spending all that time carving people up?' Daphne Harding asked with a ghoulish look in her eye.

'I doubt if he actually *enjoys* it.' Kate felt mildly shocked. 'But he enjoys making people well. That's his job, so the carving up, as you call it, is the means to that end.'

The midmorning drinks trolley arrived, and Daphne was quickly diverted by the business of deciding what kind of biscuit to have. Making sure that Zelda gave her a spouted cup so that she could manage from her side-on position, Kate went to intercept the physiotherapist, Fay Ross, who had followed the trolley in. Fay had come to treat Irene Arley. 'Mr Brown has written her up for intensive chest expansion exercises,' she told Kate, who had the task of explaining to Irene what Fay intended to do.

'Just go ahead,' Irene said in her monotone voice, speaking to where she thought Fay was standing, 'but Kate will have to tell me what to do or not to do, or you won't get any sense out of me!' She didn't want to be disturbed, poor woman, and Kate felt sorry for her. Physio so soon after surgery took some enduring. The treatment went well, but it took some time. During it two patients were wheeled down to X-Ray, others returned from it and the porters arrived to take Donna to Theatre.

Released at last, Kate took over some of the paperwork from Chloe, then had a word with a social worker who was anxious about the discharge of a patient fitted with a colostomy bag. All too soon it was lunchtime, and she was checking diet sheets, then sprinting up to the canteen for her own lunch, thinking, as she did so, that it was just as well she and her mother had decided not to try to meet. And tonight, she thought, back in the ward at the start of the quiet hour, she was meeting Clive. He was going to call for her just after seven o'clock.

It was strange how—although she was still fond of

him—he no longer had the power to excite her. There had been a time, and not so long ago either, when she'd been crazy about him, and he about her. It had been the day-to-day living together that had spoilt things, she thought. Their ways were different, and once they'd started arguing and fault-finding, the passion had flown out of the window along with the magic. Now, though, they could meet as friends and no longer have to pretend.

What would living with Lucas be like? As this thought impinged like a little arrow straight to the heart, she quickly pulled it out. She would never know, she would never find out, Lucas had warned her off.

He arrived on the ward just after visiting, Chloe doing the honours. Kate was at the ward desk, getting together the casenotes of recently discharged patients for sending down to Records. The ward desk was a vantage point for seeing most of what was going on, and as it was near Barbara Royle's bed, Kate couldn't help but hear what he was saying to her—explaining that, although he had managed to save her breast, he felt she should have a course of chemotherapy once her wound had healed. 'We've got the tumour away, no doubt about that, so it's just a precautionary measure, and one we advise in most cases where the growth is other than benign.'

'Oh, I knew it was malignant,' Barbara was answering. 'The biopsy showed that, didn't it? And, of course, I'm glad I still have my breast, but I did think I'd just need tablets afterwards, not actual chemotherapy. It brings you down, doesn't it, makes you sick and everything?'

'Not always, and we have something to help with that.' Chloe was adding her piece.

'And the man to reassure you—' Lucas's chair was scraping back '—is our oncology consultant, Fergus Lord. I'll ask him to come and see you tomorrow when you're feeling a little better, he can explain all the pros and cons far better than I can.'

There was a murmur of assent from Barbara, and now Lucas and Chloe were moving to Daphne Harding who had her husband with her. There was more talk there, and probably reassurance, and then they were moving off. If Lucas had noticed Kate, which she didn't think he had, he gave no sign of it. He wasn't stopping for tea either but, then, most likely Chloe, with her instinct for gauging the doctor's moods, had sussed out his wish to be gone.

'And it's time *you* were off,' Chloe told Kate just before five. 'It's a filthy night, raining enough to sink a battleship. I hope you've got your car!' Kate hadn't, but a few minutes later, hurrying along Princes Parade, she found that, as usual, Chloe had exaggerated. Certainly it was raining, but not especially hard, just enough to make the wide road reflect the traffic lights, enough to slant across the streetlamps like spray from a shower jet. In the more narrow enclave of Bridge Street water gurgled into the drains, and in front of Lew's shop stood Lucas's Audi, its tail-light gleaming red.

So he was shopping again, was he? Kate drew abreast of the car. Through the rain-streaked shop window she could see him buying fruit, dipping into his pocket for money, chatting to Lew. She was about to pass by when Lew spotted her and beckoned. She went into the shop, glad of the excuse to do so, her heart thumping like mad. 'I've got your box made up, love.' Lew was referring to the fruit and veg she'd ordered.

'I'll carry it up for you, if you'll hang on a sec!' He was looking at Kate, who was looking at Lucas. 'You two know each other?' he enquired with a wink.

'We're colleagues, and I'll take Miss Maybury's box up to her flat,' Lucas injected smoothly, looking round for it.

'It's here, sir.' Lew passed it to him and Kate, amazed at the way things were moving, managed to protest.

'But there's no need. It's not heavy, I can manage it myself!'

'I dare say you can.' Lucas held the box in front of him like a tray. 'But you must allow me to do my Sir Galahad act... Please, follow me!' He strode to the door, which Lew opened for him, winking again. 'Now, that's what I like to see—a lady being treated right, you don't often see it these days.'

Once the street door was unlocked and the light switched on, Lucas went first up the steep stairs. 'If I fall backwards, you can catch me!' he joked, whilst Kate, glad that she wasn't in front, giving him a view of her legs, babbled on about it being lucky that she'd seen him in Lew's.

'You see,' she went on before he could answer, 'my mother called here this morning to leave some things for me, along with the deaf-blind pamphlet I told you about. I couldn't get away to meet her, but when I rang her last night she promised she'd bring it.'

'Great. Thanks. I'm grateful, believe me!' Lucas's voice had an echoing quality. The narrow wooden stairs were sandwiched between thick walls, making getting to the flat a little like climbing the inside of a chimney. 'Test of fitness, that!' Lucas said at the top, perhaps trying, as Kate was, to dispel the faint embarrassment that hung about them.

Lucas was so different away from the hospital, so different too from the man at the stables, more like the man on the heath under the trees. Kate's thoughts ran riot, seeming to scorch her skin as she fitted the key into the flat door and heard Lucas say, 'Want me to come in and put this somewhere for you?'

'If you would, please, then I'll give you the pamphlet.' The door swung open, emitting, as it always did, a faint smell of damp and of greengroceries seeping up from the shop. 'There's a kitchen at the back.' She led the way across the thin-carpeted sitting room to the alcove kitchen, where he sat the box down on the worktop by the sink.

'Mission accomplished!'

'It was good of you, thanks. I'll just find the leaflet for you.' She sounded stiff and formal, and her tongue felt leaden. 'I expect it'll be in the bedroom with some other things my mother brought.' She went off to look and found it on top of a pile of clothes dumped on the bed in a long, white envelope addressed to 'Lucas Brown'.

'Here you are,' she said, going into the sitting room, where she found Lucas standing by the window, looking down into the lamplit street. In no sense had he made himself at home, and by that she meant that he hadn't sat down or roamed around, looking at her things. He was decent as well as gorgeous, she realised, and impeccably mannered, not the type, for instance, to take advantage and pounce on her here in the flat. So there was no need to feel so on tenterhooks, and certainly no reason to entertain the sneaking hope that he might just forget himself.

When he turned and smiled at her, she felt her knees turn to foam. 'Here you are,' she said again. 'Now you can start your swotting up!'

He looked at the envelope. 'Hmm, addressed to me—there's efficiency for you.'

'Efficiency runs in our family!'

'Like mother, like daughter,' he said, sliding his thumb under the envelope flap and drawing the pamphlet out. 'Every movement is illustrated.' He scanned it with interest.

'All you need to do is memorise and practise.' Kate moistened dry lips.

'Well, thanks,' he said simply, 'and thank your mother for helping me like this.' He put the pamphlet back in the envelope and the envelope in his pocket, being careful not to crease it, Kate noticed, but, then, she was noticing every single thing about him as he stood there by the rain-freckled window, rebuttoning his jacket.

Suddenly, painfully she didn't want him to go. She wanted him to stay. Surely he could stay a bit longer? She could offer him tea or coffee, or something stronger, perhaps. Clive wasn't due for an hour and a half so there was plenty of time. Surely she ought to make some gesture of friendliness? Yet even as she thought this, he said he ought to be going. 'You know how it is…things to be doing.'

'I do know.' She swallowed and smiled, but neither of them moved or looked anywhere but at each other. The room stilled, filled with expectant quietness. Even the rain flurrying against the window did so without sound. The space between them became enlivened, electrically charged. Neither heard the sound of footsteps on the stairs. Neither was aware of the outside world till the ringing of the doorbell broke the silence.

'I must have left the street door open!' Kate gasped, and spun round. 'It must be Lew with something I've forgotten!' But as she opened the flat door, her eyes alighted not on Lew's squat shape but on the lanky, raincoated form of Clive, his hair darkened with damp, carrying a sheaf of pink carnations across his chest like a staff.

'*Clive!*'

'Yes, I know I'm early, but I didn't think you'd mind. I can wait, you don't have to rush or anything.' He handed her the flowers, stepping forward as she opened the door more widely. It was then that he saw Lucas a few paces behind, hovering like a bodyguard, and his fair-skinned face went red. 'Oh, dear, I didn't realise you had company...' he began.

Lucas smiled affably. 'I was just about to leave.' He glanced at Kate who, clutching her flowers, introduced the two men.

'Lucas, this is Clive—Clive Mantel—a friend from London. Clive, meet Lucas Brown, a surgeon on my unit at the hospital.'

They shook hands, uttering the usual pleasantries, Clive recovering his poise, Lucas, who had never lost his, making for the door. 'Well, goodnight, then. Enjoy your evening, and thank you again for this.' He patted his pocket, looking at Kate, then opened the door and went out, leaving her and Clive listening to the thud of his feet going down the wooden stairs.

'Did I arrive at a bad time?' Clive asked, following Kate into the kitchen, where she searched for a vase for his flowers.

'No, just early,' she said, adding not a single word more.

'Is he the current boyfriend?' Clive stooped to retrieve the elastic band that had leapt from the flowers when Kate had stripped the paper off.

'No, just a friendly colleague.' Kate was beginning to relent. 'These are really lovely, Clive.' She buried her nose in the flowers which now sat in a wide glass jug. 'How about taking them through in the sitting room? Then I'll make us some tea, and you can tell me where we're bound for tonight so that I know what to put on.' It was no good, she told herself, feeling miffed with him. It would only make a bad start to their evening, and she did want to go out.

'I came here straight from work,' he explained, when they were drinking their tea. 'It didn't seem worthwhile tramping back to my rooms in this rain.'

'Didn't you have your car, then? Don't you drive in to work?' Kate asked, surprised.

'No, I walk. I like the exercise, and it wasn't raining first thing. The only thing is, we'll have to rely on taxis tonight.'

'We don't have to—we can use my car,' Kate said promptly. 'It's sitting in its shed at the back here. Taxis cost the earth.'

'Yes, I know they do, so if you don't mind getting your car out...' The slight pucker between Clive's brow disappeared like smoke. He was relieved, Kate could see that, and she had the unworthy thought that he had subtly guided and manoeuvred her into making the suggestion she had. Clive wasn't mean, but he watched expenses—a side-effect of his accountancy job. 'Because if you do mind—' he was still going on about it '—I can easily fetch the BMW from Elvington Road while you're getting changed.'

'And get wet?'

'Well...yes.'

'What's the point?' Kate bent to pick up the tray. 'I like driving, I know the town and you don't. Anyway, where are we going? I need to know what to wear.'

'I thought the leisure centre out at Coe Fen.' Clive took the tray from her hands. 'I've been hearing about it from one of the clerks at Barchesters. As well as a skating rink, there's a heated pool and restaurant facilities, not that we want to eat there tonight but we may as well have a look.'

'It's a fairly new complex. It wasn't around when I was training,' Kate called from the bedroom. 'Are we going there first?'

'I thought so, yes.' Clive was washing the cups. 'We could go on a sort of recce, then come back into the town for supper—to the Red Lion, if you like.'

'Sounds good to me!' So my black trousers, she was thinking, and my fuchsia top, plus a long mac for ploughing round to the back yard to get the car. Half an hour later, on the point of doing this, she told Clive to wait inside the street door. 'I'll bring the car round; you won't like the mud in the yard!'

He insisted on going with her, though, and together they tramped past the shop façade, up the drive at the side and round to the yard, where a sagging shed housed Kate's white car and Lew's green van.

'Bit primitive, isn't it?' Clive leapt a pothole awash with water.

'I was lucky to get a garage of any kind.' Kate made her way to the shed, feeling for her keys, cautioning Clive to stand clear whilst she backed the car out.

Once this had been accomplished he got in and they rocked down the drive, the windscreen wipers wagging furiously, Clive doing his best—or so Kate thought—to bite back further derogatory remarks. He hadn't changed, she realised. He still liked everything neat and tidy, yet another side effect of his job.

'This is like old times,' he said, as she turned out into the street, heading for the bridge and the tree-lined road beyond that led to Coe Fen.

'Well, not quite. I've never driven you before,' Kate pointed out, changing into top gear. They were on the north side of the river now, passing the block of flats that was Maitland House ablaze with lights on their right. Which flat was Lucas's? Were he and Claire together, cooking supper, being cosy? Oh, forget them. Let them get on with it, she thought with a prick of misery.

'You drive really well, Kate.'

Clive was trying to be nice, making up for being critical earlier on. She felt a rush of affection for him, a touch of *déjà vu*. For heaven's sake, he was taking her out for the evening. The least she could do was forget about Lucas and concentrate on him. 'Thanks for the compliment,' she said smilingly. 'I like being behind the wheel, and I need a car down here to be really mobile. I can get home to Cruse Cottage in twenty minutes, which beats the bus or train any day.'

'Makes you more independent,' Clive said thoughtfully, then added. 'You've changed, you know.'

'Perhaps we both have.' Kate braked at the lights. 'We've not seen one another for nearly a year, no one stays the same. Anyway, let's just enjoy ourselves.'

And that's what they did, spending over an hour at the leisure centre, then coming back into the town to eat leek soup and sole *corbière* at the Red Lion on Market Hill. Kate wondered if she ought to offer to pay her half of the bill, but when she mentioned this to Clive as they drove home, he said his expense account would cover it, leaving her feeling not too surprised but a shade uncomfortable.

'Next time we'll go Dutch,' she told him when they were driving home.

'Next time we could spend the whole evening at the centre.' Clive was in happy mood. 'We could skate till we drop, then eat at that whole food café there. We could probably do something each night of the week in that place.'

'I'm on late duty some evenings.' Kate filtered carefully into the stream of traffic at the conduit roundabout. 'And then there's days off. I go home for those, and they don't always fall at a weekend now that I'm rostered with the permanent staff.'

'Marcus and I go back to London at the weekends.' Clive shifted beside her. 'I like to keep an eye on the flat and he rejoins his wife.'

Kate took all this in with a modicum of relief. She wanted to meet up with Clive—of course she did—but not every evening, or even alternative evenings. She needed some time to herself.

'Do you have to go home on your days off?' he asked her presently.

'No, I just like to.' She was making the right-hand turn into Elvington Road, then slowing to a crawl, asking him what number to stop at.

'Oh, sorry. Number twenty-five, that's it by the lamp.' Once the car had halted at the kerb he released his seat belt, head bent low. 'So, how shall we leave things?' he asked. 'You'll have a mobile. Can I ring you on that?'

'Good idea,' she said, relieved not to have to decide on a date straight away. Scribbling her number down on a scrap of paper she produced from her bag, she asked him only to ring early in the morning or late at night. 'Mobiles aren't allowed on at the hospital, but I'll be very glad to hear from you, Clive.' She added this because he was sitting beside her looking glum, emanating the sort of silence that meant he wasn't pleased.

'I'll ring you tomorrow, if only for a chat.' He leaned sideways and kissed her cheek. There was a blast of cold air as he opened the door and stepped onto the pavement, then he was moving swiftly up the long garden path, waving to her from the porch.

In bed that night Kate went over the events of the evening, starting with Lucas coming up to the flat. She had felt thrilled to have him there, prickly with longing. She had wanted to keep him there. He'd felt it too, she was sure he had. There had been about him the same aura of need that she'd glimpsed just before he'd kissed her that Sunday on the heath. Would he have reached out for her this evening if Clive hadn't broken the spell? She felt he would have, she was sure he would have, so perhaps it was possible that he and Claire weren't passionately linked, or even that they were cooling off. Then she blushed with shame in the darkness. Get real, she told herself.

CHAPTER EIGHT

KATE'S mobile rang at six forty-five next morning and, yes, it was Clive, apologising for being offhand when he'd left her the previous evening. 'Of *course* you like to go home on your days off. I was being unreasonable.'

Kate, who had scarcely noticed, said it was quite all right. 'Actually, my next days off are Friday and Saturday, so I'll be driving home on Thursday night.'

'Well, then…' There was a brief pause. 'Can we meet up on Monday night? We could go to the leisure centre and skate—if you want to, of course.'

'Sounds fine to me.' Kate was shivering. She'd been under the shower when he'd rung. Now, wrapped in an inadequate towel, she hoped he wouldn't be long, but he was going on about skating boots and how he was buying a new pair 'from that sports shop in St Andrew's Street. I expect the centre hire out skates, but I'd sooner have my own'.

'My mother brought mine yesterday,' Kate said between chattering teeth, trying to say that she ought to be going but having to hang on whilst Clive told her he was just about to set out on his jog. On a raw and dark November morning, he has to be crazy, she thought, free at last to get into her clothes.

Later, on the ward, at the tail end of the medicine round, it fell to Kate to escort Fergus Lord, the oncology consultant, to Barbara Royle's bed. Small, dapper and with a bouncing gait, he bobbed along at her side.

116

He had been studying Barbara's notes in which Lucas had included a diagram of her wound 'which will have to heal completely before I start treatment'. He plopped down on the chair Kate pulled out.

Barbara, in some ways an intimidating woman, gave him a measured look. 'That is if I decide to have the treatment,' she said with emphasis.

Fergus looked momentarily startled. 'Let me explain what I have in mind,' he said, rather more gently. He went on at length, whilst Kate, mindful of other patients' needs, was relieved when Chloe appeared at the ward doors, making beckoning signs. With a muttered apology she crossed over to her, thankful to be free.

'There's no need to stay there with him.' Chloe blew out her cheeks. 'He goes on and on like a running tap.' She went on to tell Kate about a new patient who was coming in at noon. 'An incisional hernia case, name of Carmen Harridew. She had a pelvic colectomy four years ago. These are her notes, all we have at present. She's to go in the side-ward first. Lucas Brown is likely to be along to see her during the afternoon, when he'll probably discharge the appendix case.'

On her way to the first of the side-wards with the student nurse, Karen Johnson, Kate saw Donna coming out of the lavatories, walking carefully but looking happy in her bright red dressing-gown.

'I feel great,' she said, when Kate asked how she was. 'I can't believe I had all that pain. My stomach's sore, but not all that much. I've got strips, not stitches, you know.'

The sealed dressing was displayed to Karen and the two girls giggled together, Donna with restraint, holding her abdomen, but clearly enjoying the company of someone not so very much older than herself. Kate felt every one of her twenty-six years as, taking Karen with her, she prepared the side-ward for the arrival of Carmen Harridew.

She arrived on the stroke of twelve midday—a big freckle-faced woman of forty-eight with dyed red hair. Her hernia, which was enormous and causing her great discomfort, contained the whole of her transverse colon and much of her small intestine.

Her husband—a burly, brutish type—complained about the time she'd been on the waiting list. 'How would you like to walk about with that thing poking out of your belly?' he asked, treating Kate to a baleful stare as though it was all her fault.

'We'll have trouble with him, he's that sort,' Chloe predicted darkly when, with Carmen settled and her husband gone, Kate escaped to early lunch.

There was a veritable stream of visitors that after-noon. Irene Arley's sister came, and the two 'con-versed'. Then shortly after three o'clock Lucas joined them, said something to the sister and, taking Irene's left hand, began signing on it. He wasn't very quick and kept glancing at Kate's pamphlet lying open on the bed, but he was certainly making a concerted and brave effort for, as Kate knew well, the first try was daunting and confusing for both signer and recipient. But Irene was answering and looking delighted. So was the sister, Kate noticed as she flicked glances at them, wishing she could join in.

'He's learnt her way of signing,' Daphne Harding said from her lying-on-the-side position as Kate went to pour her some water.

'Looks like it.' Kate didn't turn round as she was directly opposite them now.

'But, then, of course, he's an intelligent man,'

Barbara Royle put in, feeling no happier after her talk with Fergus Lord. 'All I want to do,' she'd told Kate earlier, 'is look after my own body without other people taking it over.'

'There are times when that isn't wise, Mrs Royle.' Kate had chosen her words carefully. 'Sometimes things happen outside our control then we need expertise help.'

Barbara hadn't replied, and Kate wondered what she would decide about the proposed chemotherapy. She wondered what she herself would decide, given the same set of circumstances. It was impossible to say, impossible to tell from the outside looking in. All she knew was that she'd trust Lucas completely—if necessary with her life.

'Whoops, he's coming over!' Daphne, it seemed, could see round corners, or round Kate's slim shape, for the next moment Lucas was there, nodding at her, smiling at Daphne, drawing the curtains between her bed and Barbara Royle's. 'You've not come to turn me over, I hope, because if it's all the same to you, I'd rather be left as I am, thank you very much!' Daphne's cheek, Kate knew, was to hide her fear of being hurt when she was moved, and her eye fastened warily on Lucas as he sat on the edge of the bed.

'No, I'll leave all that to our nurses, Mrs Harding.' He smiled down at her. 'But I've not seen you since your operation, and I wanted you to know that everything went very well, and you've nothing to worry about.'

'All thanks to you.' She was grinning now. 'And call me Daphne. After the view you had of my rear end yesterday, we can't stand on ceremony!'

Lucas passed on that one by assuring her that

Daphne was his favourite name. He also told her she was a splendid patient and that he was very pleased with her.

'I bet you say that to all the girls!' she said, but by then he was making his way up the ward to have a word with Donna's mother, who had been trying to attract his attention from her daughter's bed.

After that Chloe annexed him to go and talk to Carmen Harridew's husband. There was no chance for Kate to do more than glimpse him.

On Thursday Peter told her Lucas was on leave until Monday. 'He's spending a few days with his father.'

She wondered if she would see him on Friday when she went riding, but although Hercules's loose box was empty, there was no sign of Lucas on the heath and, on returning to the stables, Iris told her that the horse was being exercised by Mr Vernon. 'He always takes him out once a day when Mr Brown's not here,' she said.

Kate was furious with herself for being disappointed. 'How stupid can you get?' she muttered, tramping home in the bitter cold, wishing she'd stayed at home herself.

Then on Saturday morning, shopping with her mother in Cletford high street, she spotted him on the zebra crossing, walking slowly at the side of an older man who was walking with a stick. Paula saw him, too, or saw his companion. 'There's Gervase Brown!' she exclaimed. 'Out on a Saturday, in all this crush. I suppose that's the son?'

Inevitably they met and after that it was all introductions and a criss-crossing of arms for shaking hands. Then Gervase Brown, warmly clad in an overcoat with an astrakhan collar, said he and Lucas were on their way to the Rutland Hotel 'for something to warm us up. How about joining us?' He was looking at Kate, his shrewd blue eyes missing very little as she smiled back at him, tucking a strand of tawny hair back inside her hood.

Paula and Lucas kept their sizing-up of one another till they were sitting in the cocktail lounge of the hotel with their drinks in front of them. Lucas, thanking Paula for lending him the deaf-blind pamphlet, said he'd return it as soon as possible.

'No need,' Paula said briskly. 'Kate and I never use it.'

'And judging from the way he's been practising on me, he'll soon be top of the class,' Gervase grumbled good-naturedly, swallowing a mouthful of brandy and soda.

'Speed is of the essence,' Paula said. 'To be slow is wearisome for the recipient.'

'I'll remember that,' Lucas said meekly, and Kate gave him a sidelong look. In no way was Lucas a meek man, so he must have his tongue in his cheek—not that her mother would notice this, she was too intent on giving him a speedy demonstration on her own splayed-out hand, to the interest of two people at a nearby table, who probably thought he was deaf.

After a little more round-the-table talk, Gervase asked Paula if she could fix him up with some more acupuncture treatment. She recommended a new clinic on the outskirts of the town, and whilst they were discussing this Lucas asked Kate if her boyfriend had gone back to London.

'Yes, he has.' She nodded. 'Just for the weekend. He'll be back tomorrow night. Clive's an accountant with a firm in the City, and he's down here on an audit with his senior partner. He's likely to be here for another month. And he's an ex-boyfriend,' she added. 'We were together once, but it didn't work out.'

'And now he's back in the picture again, is he?'

'Well, yes, but only because he's been sent to where I happen to be. We're still friends and we feel it'll be fun to meet and go around together whilst he's here. When we split up it was on good terms, there was no awful row.' And I'm explaining too much, Kate thought. He won't want to hear all this.

Lucas half turned to face her, a small smile curving his mouth. 'I'm always a bit sceptical about these amicable partings,' he said. 'Surely one of the parties has to be aggrieved, or hurt, or at best left with enough hope to plan a comeback at some point.'

'Well, that wasn't the case with Clive and me,' Kate began, then stopped in mid-sentence as she spotted a couple—a man and a girl, both hatless, both windblown and glowing, both wearing padded jackets— bearing down on their table.

Lucas, following her glance, rose to his feet. 'Claire, Hugh, so you've found us at last!' He stepped forward and greeted them both, whilst Claire bent to his father, who was trying to get up. Both newcomers were introduced to Paula, and Hugh Jevons to Kate. 'You won't have met Kate, Mrs Maybury's daughter.' Lucas was leaving no one out.

'We glimpsed one another through a curtain of rain last weekend at the stables!' Hugh Jevons's thin, hard hand met Kate's in a painful grip. With everyone hovering, Lucas cast about for more chairs. He was stopped by Kate, however, who said she and her mother ought to be going.

'We've still got some shopping to do, and we're going out this afternoon, but the drink came at just the right time. Mr Brown, thank you for asking us.' She smiled across at Gervase who was reaching for his stick.

'It made all the difference.' Paula stepped back from her chair which was promptly taken by Claire. Her cousin, however, rather more polite, waited until Kate and her mother had said their goodbyes before seating himself.

In the cold windy street once more and diving for cover into the chemist's, Paula asked Kate why they'd had to make such a quick getaway. 'Surely there was no need? It was just getting interesting.'

'It would have been awkward to stay once the Jevonses arrived. We'd have been in the way,' Kate said, following her mother over to the bath accessories section.

'I don't see why.' Paula selected a toothbrush from the stand and dropped it into her wire basket. 'Oh, come on, let's get home, shall we?' she growled, as someone trod on her heel. 'I'm not in the mood for any more pushing around.'

To this Kate agreed willingly enough, but once at home in front of the fire, with lunch trays on their knees, Paula asked about Claire. 'She's the girl Lucas is involved with, isn't she? Gervase mentioned her to me once. Her family live out at Betchworth. He knows her father who's a chiropractor at the private clinic he used to use.'

'Oh,' Kate said, digesting this. 'I meet her on and off at the hospital, of course. She's the ortho sister.'

'Looks competent.'

'She is.'

'Pretty, too.'

Kate wished that her mother would talk about something else, and in a bid to bring this about she said, 'Hadn't we better hurry up if we want to get to the Odeon in time for the start of the film?'

They enjoyed the film and their tea at the Gold Cup Café, where they indulged in muffins and Suffolk honey. All the same, driving back to Seftonbridge at half past eight that evening, Kate knew she wasn't sorry to be returning to her flat, and independent life.

Sunday on the ward followed the usual pattern, with the hospital chaplain making an early appearance, chatting to the patients who were well enough, including the ebullient Daphne Harding who, at six day's post-op, no longer had to view life and people lying on her side. 'It's been a bit weird, but I'm getting on fine now,' she told him when he enquired, but she didn't regale him with lurid details, much to Kate's relief.

The aloof Barbara Royle smiled a greeting at him, then returned to her newspaper. Fully dressed, she was sitting at the side of her bed. 'The sooner I get back to normal the better,' she had told Kate earlier on.

Out of the half-dozen or so patients the Reverend Scarfe spoke to, Irene Arley appreciated him the most, for once Kate had told him about her disability, he picked up her hand and displayed a complete mastery of hand signing. 'Unfortunately, to be both deaf and blind isn't as rare as one might imagine,' he remarked to a surprised Kate when she plied him with coffee in the office before he departed.

Sunday afternoons always brought more visitors than usual, many coming from farther afield than even the outlying fen villages. By four o'clock beds and lockers were awash with flowers, fruit and magazines, most of which had to be watered, tidied away or picked up. Chloe, who had come on duty with the afternoon shift, swore quietly under her breath as a small child was sick all over the floor.

It was nearly six before Kate came off shift. Clive rang her shortly after nine, confirming their date for the next evening. 'I'll have the car this time. I'll pick you up at seven precisely,' he said.

He was as good as his word, his red BMW sliding to a halt outside Lew's on the stroke of seven next evening. Kate, with her jeans tucked into her boots and a warm fleece taking the place of her jacket, slid into the passenger seat. With not too much traffic to negotiate they were at the leisure centre, lacing themselves into skating boots, well within half an hour.

'This is great!' Clive enthused as they moved onto the ice. 'I would never have expected to find anything like it outside London.'

Kate nodded without speaking, for she was concentrating hard. Skating was as easy as breathing to Clive but she took time to get into her stride. He had her by the hand, and this was unusual. On the South London rink he had always shot away, leaving her to her own devices. Maybe he's getting more considerate in his old age, she thought, smiling to herself as he steered her competently round a cat-suited youth, who was showing off his figure-skating skills and taking up most of the rink.

Even so, she sensed in Clive a wish to be off—a wish to be trying out something spectacular himself. He was a talented skater and had won countless competitions so she could in no way match up to him. She also felt like she was spoiling his fun a little so she persuaded him to go off by himself. 'I've got my ice-legs now. We can go round again when you've had a good go. I can tell you're dying to!'

'Are you sure?' His hand loosened round hers.

'Couldn't be more so,' she said.

'Well, all right. I'll be back in a few minutes. In the meantime…' he did a small circle round her '…don't go talking to any strange men!'

'I'll try to restrain myself.' She laughed, watching him move away, slowly at first then lengthening his glide, flashing across the rink in a zig-zag movement, weaving effortlessly in and out of other groups. Then, finding more space in the centre of the rink, he began to execute complicated turns, his long thin body perfectly balanced, his skating style reminding Kate of the many times she had watched him taking part in competitions.

Sinking down on one of the tiered seats that surrounded the rink, her eye passed over other skaters, whose numbers wre increasing fast. From this slightly raised level she spotted Claire and her cousin, Hugh, on the far side of the rink, skating separately but side by side. Where was Lucas? Her heart jumped. Surely he was here as well? Her eyes searched the moving mass of skaters, but there was no sign of him. He was probably on call, she decided, or maybe there had been some sort of emergency at the hospital. As for Claire and Hugh, they were drawing to a standstill, turning to watch Clive who was drawing a small audience. People were clapping on all sides. This didn't surprise Kate because once on the ice Clive stepped right out of his self-conscious, slightly stuffy image and emerged as a star in his own right. But almost without realising she was doing so, she was still on the lookout for Lucas, which was why she didn't see Claire and Hugh skating towards her till they were coming off the ice.

'We noticed you skating earlier, then spotted you sitting here,' Claire said as they seated themselves, one on each side of her.

A little surprised at her over-friendliness, Kate smiled a greeting. Longing to ask where Lucas was, she managed to restrain herself. Claire might think it odd, and in any case Hugh was addressing her.

'Claire,' he said a little heavily, 'is entranced by your friend's skating skills.'

'Oh, he's an expert.' She could at least expound on that. 'He's won all sorts of competitions at our club in London.'

'I'd love to partner him!' Claire enthused, clambering to her feet and clapping as Clive went into a spin, whirling around on one skate.

'When he comes off I'll introduce you,' Kate said, amazed at Claire's exuberance. She was usually so buttoned-up.

'Looks as though he's just concluding his act.' Hugh bent forward to adjust one of his skates.

'Yes, he is.' Kate waved frantically—not that Clive hadn't already seen her. He was coming in at speed, probably wondering who she was with, for he hadn't met either Claire or Hugh. As soon as he reached them Kate performed the introductions, Claire wasting no time in asking him to partner her.

He looked embarrassed and hesitant and—Kate noticed with a certain amount of glee—not very pleased. 'I've left Kate for rather a long time already, Miss Jevons.' He made to take off his woolly hat.

'Oh, Kate will be all right. Hugh will look after her.' Claire pressed on, unabashed. 'I'm no novice skater.

I've won competitions *and* I'm in the county ice hockey team!' She smiled steadily up into Clive's face, not beguilingly but with a hint of authority, practically ordering him to take her on.

Feeling it was time she eased the situation, Kate insisted that she would be perfectly happy on her own, sitting there watching them.

They went off then, joined hands and began to skate, drawing the attention of the crowd in no time, some of whom cleared a space for them.

'Your cousin is ace,' Kate remarked to Hugh, watching Claire's darting, quicksilver movements, so perfectly attuned to Clive's.

Hugh grunted assent. 'Yes, she is…far too good for me. I'm what you might call a pedestrian skater. I do get *some* practice in New Zealand, but not all that much.'

'New Zealand?' Kate's attention was caught.

'That's where I live now!'

'Goodness…what a long way away!'

He turned to smile at her. 'Not these days, not by flying time. I get to England several times a year.'

'What part of New Zealand? Is your job there? Were you sent to work there?'

Hugh laughed at that. 'You make me sound like an exiled convict,' he laughed. 'I live in Auckland, North Island. My business is in wine.'

How grand, Kate was thinking, going on to enquire if he'd been there long, and once again his reply surprised her. 'I went over in my gap year, renounced university and decided to stay there. In all I've been there close on twenty years.'

So… Kate was doing her sums. He'd be about thirty-eight. 'Claire must have missed you,' she finished.

'I suppose she did. I like to think she did, although as children we fought like cats and dogs, jealousy rearing its head, mostly, I'm afraid, on my part.

'Perhaps,' Hugh said, 'we should be taking a turn round that rink, even though we may not...' he glanced over at the swirling Claire and Clive '...be in the exhibitionist class. How about it, Kate?'

'I'd like that,' she said, so off they went, he catching her hand in his. He was nice, she decided, an attractive man, far nicer than his cousin, who without doubt had appropriated Clive without so much as a by your leave. Claire, she decided, would always get what she wanted. Other people's hurts and feelings wouldn't be her concern.

Kate and Hugh stayed on the ice till Claire and Clive—to the sound of clapping—made their way to the side. Both seemed exhilarated by their session, and Claire was all for them making a foursome and having supper back in the town. Clive was quick to veto this, however, much to Kate's relief. 'Kate and I are eating here at the whole food café—à deux.' He smiled, putting a fairly obvious emphasis on the last two words.

'I'm glad you said that,' Kate told him, after the four of them had parted company. 'With Claire you have to make yourself very plain.'

'I didn't want to be stuck with them for the rest of the evening. What's the cousin like?' he asked.

'Nice to talk to, nice to skate with, he works in New Zealand,' she said. This evinced no interest from Clive but, once seated in the whole food café, he commented on Claire's skating skills.

'She's not bad,' he said, 'but I've partnered better.'

Dear Clive. Kate sighed, happily spooning up lentil soup. 'She's Lucas Brown's girlfriend,' she explained.

'You remember him, don't you? He was at the flat when you called for me last week.'

'Of course I remember him.' He raised clear eyes to Kate's. 'I thought he was *your* boyfriend.'

'No way.' She swallowed convulsively. 'I told you so at the time.' She held his look and managed to smile, but was relieved when he changed the subject and began to talk about people they both knew in London.

'I suppose,' he said, thoughtfully buttering a piece of roll, 'you wouldn't consider coming up with me one weekend? You'd be able to catch up with some of your nursing friends. We could stay at the flat...as friends, of course. I'm not trying to welsh on our agreement, or anything like that.' His voice trailed off as an embarrassed Kate shook her head.

'Clive, I'm not sure if that would be a good idea—meeting in London.'

'Why?' For a second his face hardened as he said, 'We're meeting here, now.'

'I know, but this is just an interlude, isn't it? It suits us both, it's an expediency, a one-off, we agreed on that, just for the time you're here!'

Clive's angry flush faded, and Kate crossed her fingers, sitting back in her chair as their waitress put platters of green salad and jacket potatoes in front of them.

'All right, I'll remember the ground rules.' Clive picked up his knife and fork. 'And if I don't I'm sure you'll remind me of them.' His long, fair lashes were down, screening her off from him, and Kate found herself holding her breath. 'However,' he said, still looking down, still busy with knife and fork, 'there is just *one* thing I hope you'll meet me on.'

'Oh?' Good Lord, what was coming now? Kate braced herself.

'Marcus would like us both to dine with him one evening at River Lawns. He'll invite his cousin, a Miss Rymer, to join us. She's a teacher at the Cathedral Park School, lives at Ely. Marcus is my senior partner, Kate, so I hope you won't say no.'

'Oh, good heavens, Clive, of course I won't,' a relieved Kate all but gushed. 'I'd love to come. How kind of Mr Brandt. Even if I'm on duty when he asks us, I'll get someone to swap with me!'

'That's great!' Clive was appeased, and showed it, smiling into Kate's eyes. 'I'll try to let you know in good time. I knew you wouldn't let me down!'

You didn't, you felt I easily might, Kate was thinking to herself, but for the rest of the evening there was no discord, no hint of an argument. She really enjoyed herself and she felt that Clive did too. Even saying goodnight in the car outside Lew's didn't prove a problem—a swift hug and a 'thank you' breathed into her ear was exactly right, she thought.

CHAPTER NINE

THE next few days saw many patient changes on Guthrie Ward. Irene Arley and Daphne Harding remained, though, so did Carmen Harridew. Carmen had progressed well after surgery, but unfortunately, just as Lucas was on the point of discharging her, she developed flu and had to be moved back into side-ward one.

Walter Harridew, always on the lookout for trouble, vowed to sue the hospital. 'My wife came here to be made well, not to go down with an infection!' he said angrily to Kate, having marched into the main ward to tackle her at the desk.

It was Thursday, mid-afternoon, the peak time for visiting. Outside a sleet-driven rain was lashing against the windows. Inside, with the lights full on, a fuggy heat emanated from wet coats and parkas. Several visitors had coughs and colds. Chloe had gone off duty, feeling unwell, leaving Kate in charge and at the mercy of complainants, one of whom was Mr Harridew.

'Carmen is much better today.' Kate did her best to placate him.

'I should hope so!' he spluttered, 'but it should never have happened. She should be at home with me now, not coughing her lungs up in here, straining and heaving and probably rupturing herself!'

'Her surgical condition is just fine,' Kate said, perhaps not quite as calmly as she might have, but there were several other visitors queuing behind him, wanting to speak to her. As she moved to one side he blocked her path, thrusting his face into hers.

'I want to speak to the sister, or to my wife's consultant. I'm not leaving here until I do!'

'Mr Brown is in Theatre, and will be until late—'

'And Sister's got flu,' Karen piped up from the desk, unintentionally adding fuel to Mr Harridew's fire.

'Well, there you are, then.' He puffed out his cheeks. 'The whole place is rife with germs, most probably brought in by staff! It's a disgrace, I say, a positive disgrace. I shall involve the press!' His voice was raised and he'd swung round to address the rest of the ward. Then he marched out of it. 'I have a business appointment, but I'll be back at six.'

'When he'll have his gun with him!' May Boughton said, but although Kate laughed, she wasn't really amused. There was only herself, May, Nurse Liu and Karen on duty. She herself was working a double shift.

Expecting Peter Graves to look in on the three patients due for surgery next day, she was startled to see Lucas appear at the office doorway at a little after six o'clock. 'Peter's got raging toothache, face is up like a balloon,' he told her, helping himself to the relevant notes before she could get to her feet. 'It's all right, I can manage, you stay where you are,' he muttered, sweeping into the ward, leaving her feeling a little brushed-off, yet relieved to be left to the daily chore of writing up the nursing report. He'd be bringing the notes back again so she'd see him then, Kate thought with a little lift of her spirits. Just then she became aware of someone talking outside Carmen Harridew's side-ward door.

Looking out she saw Walter Harridew, leaning against the wall, speaking on his mobile phone. He was carrying on about something or other but, whatever it was, he had no business using his mobile inside the hospital. There were enough notices to this effect plastered all over the walls. Surely the man could read? Rather glad to have something on him Kate sprang into action.

'Please, switch that off, Mr Harridew. There's a payphone along the corridor if you need to make a call.'

He made a sound like a growl, his fleshy cheeks bulged and, yes, he did switch off, but brandished the phone like a weapon. 'Who do you think you are, pouncing on me, giving me orders? I'll do what I damn well like!'

'But not here in the hospital, Mr Harridew.' Lucas's calm, civil voice came over Kate's shoulder, then he passed her and approached the indignant man by the wall. 'You see,' he went on, 'mobile phones could interfere with essential life-saving equipment, put a patient's life at risk. Now, I'm quite sure you wouldn't want that, and as I'm just about to have a word with Mrs Harridew, perhaps we could go in together.' He was smiling at Walter but making his point just the same as he motioned to Kate to leave them, making a backward sweep with his hand. Thankfully Kate returned to the office, being disturbed almost at once by another visitor who said her mother—an elderly patient—had been sick all over the floor.

Kate found Lucas in the office when, the disaster having been coped with and the patient calmed, she made her way back there again. He was jerking down the blind with a testy movement. 'You can't want to look out on that,' he exclaimed. Kate presumed he meant the filthy night.

'No, I don't, though I haven't had time—' she began, but was interrupted in mid-flow.

'Not a pleasant individual, our Mr Harridew.' Lucas moved towards the door. 'All the same,' he continued, with his hand on the jamb, 'you were less than tactful in handling him, I thought.'

'What do you mean?' Kate stared back at him.

'What I say,' Lucas frowned. 'You were right to stop him using his mobile, but you all but dived on the man! At one point I thought you were about to wrest it from him and swipe him on the head with it!'

'I can't believe…' Kate faltered a little, then stood clear of the desk. 'I can't believe you said that!' Anger flushed her cheeks.

'It needed to be said.' They were facing one another like combatants again. 'We're likely to have trouble with Harridew, and needling him at this stage can only make matters worse.' Lucas made his point with care.

'I think you're making a fuss about nothing at all…nit-picking!' Kate was saying too much, letting her anger spill over, and Lucas's face went dark.

'Now, look here…' He took a step forward, and Kate unconsciously braced herself, but what he intended to say was never given voice for a scared-looking Nurse Liu appeared at the open doorway.

'It's the new patient.' She looked at Kate. 'I can't get her to take her medication. She says she can't swallow pills.'

'All right, Nurse, I'll come, if Mr Brown has finished with me now.' Her eyes flicked to Lucas who was wearing his smooth face again.

'I have, so I'll say goodnight to you both.' And with that he was off, not hurrying, in no way fleeing the scene. In fact, he was practically sauntering, scarcely moving the hem of his long white coat with the little vent at the back.

As for Kate, she still felt ill-used, but as the long evening passed she had to admit, in all fairness, that Lucas had had a point. She *had* been overly officious with Walter Harridew. She'd been glad of the chance to tell him off, to put him in the wrong after his rudeness to her earlier in the ward. Lucas wouldn't have known about that, and quite likely he had been taken to task about Carmen's condition when he'd gone into the side-ward with him. Bad feeling was catching, everyone knew that, and Kate sighed with tiredness, wishing she didn't mind quite so much, and so painfully, about what Lucas thought of her.

She took the lift when at last she came off duty at a little before ten p.m. At that time of night it wasn't so much in demand, so she didn't have long to wait before it arrived at the fourth floor and yawned back its doors. On the way down, when it halted at the second floor, about a dozen people got in, one of them being Lucas in his dark green parka, plainly bound for home. Kate swallowed convulsively, moving towards the back of the lift. For the first time ever she didn't want to see him or want him to see her but, of course, he did. The lift was well lit, and there was enough room in it for everyone to look round at everyone else.

He smiled, and moved to her side. 'You're late tonight.'

'So are you.' Kate stared fixedly at the neck of a young nurse standing in front of her.

'True enough.' They reached the ground floor and Lucas kept pace with her as they walked towards the revolving doors that would swing them out into the night. Pulling the hood of her anorak forward, Kate

wished him goodnight, glancing briefly up at him as
she made to step down the ramp.

'Haven't you got your car?' His words stopped her
midway.

'No, I haven't, I like to walk after spending hours
in a stuffy ward.' She was having to stop now to tie
her hood, which was flying back in the wind.

'But at this time of night, and in this weather!' He
sounded incredulous. 'Let me give you a lift.' He
touched her arm. 'Come on, now, let's get to the car.'

'No, I mean it.' Kate panicked, his touch and his
nearness was getting to her again, making her feel torn
between longing to stay with him and the need to get
away fast. 'I really mean it. I'd rather walk.' Pulling
away to the side, she ended up in a giant puddle,
splashing herself up to her knees. She gave a small
shriek.

'Oh, for crying out loud, what are you trying to do,
give yourself pneumonia?' Hauling her towards him,
up against him, he brought his mouth to hers with a
swift, hard, hurting pressure, bruising her lips with his
teeth. Then, keeping tight hold of her, giving her no
quarter, no possible chance of escape, he hustled her
to the car park and into his car. 'For the rough handling
I apologise!' he said harshly, closing the passenger
door.

But she'd loved it, hadn't she? Getting her breath
back, she watched him get in on his side. She was
waiting for him to kiss her again, surely he would kiss
her again. But, no, he was switching the engine on,
telling her to fasten her seat belt. 'We don't want to be
here all night, do we?' He sounded tetchy and cross.

'No, of course not.' Feeling slapped down, she
leaned to reach for her seat belt, but a smarting anger

came to her rescue and a touch of wry humour, too. Clearly he was the sort of man who never got romantic in cars, preferring to do it on hospital forecourts with staff milling about, with cars cruising along to the gates, with a hundred different eyes looking out from lighted windows as the nurses drew down blinds.

They were moving off now, then as quickly they stopped again. A small jumping-up-and-down figure was waving his arms directly in front of them, easily recognisable as Fergus Lord in the full glare of the lights.

'What the...?' Lucas opened his window as Fergus darted round to his side.

'Any chance of a lift? My car won't start...something wrong with it.'

'Oh, dear, bad luck. Of course. Get in!' Lucas opened a rear door, and the little man dived in, spotting Kate for the first time and calling her Nurse Shaftesbury. 'Hope I'm not intruding, but I needed to see—'

'Fergus, you're welcome.' Lucas was trying to stop the verbal flow. Kate wondered where Fergus Lord lived—perhaps in the same block of flats as Lucas. Yet it seemed not, for as they joined the cavalcade of traffic in Princes Parade, he began to babble about a house.

'I can be out of it by next week... A good thing, too... Far too big for me...shall let it first, then consider selling. So, if you're still of the same mind, Lucas... Up to you, of course. Since I've been spreading the word, I've had plenty of takers, but I know you said...'

'I'm interested, definitely.' Lucas sounded buffeted as he braked at the lights. 'Can we talk about this when I've dropped Kate off?'

'Please, don't bother to get out,' she said, once they were pulling up outside Lew's. She hadn't especially relished his dismissive remark, which was a far cry from his passionate insistence that she accompany him, or else, but get out he did, and so did Fergus, moving from the back of the car to the front seat, eager to start talking again.

Lucas lingered a little, unlocking Kate's door, handing back her key, their fingers grazing. 'There you are, home and dry!'

'I could have walked, I like walking, but thanks all the same… Goodnight.' Then she went in, leaving him to the verbose Fergus and their chat about the house.

Was Lucas, she wondered, thinking of moving out of his flat—the flat that Jean had once told her was next to Claire's? Perhaps she was moving with him. Perhaps their affair was to become an acknowledged living-together commitment. They might even be getting married, or would do so eventually. The thought of this clawed at her painfully. She was amazed at how much it hurt. She hardly knew him, she couldn't be in love with him, she couldn't be, she wasn't like that. It took her ages to so much as like anyone, let alone love them. But Lucas was different, he was *so* different from anyone she'd met before, and he was drawn to her, she knew that. Could he be tired of Claire, could their affair be waning? Was that why he was thinking of moving out of Maitland House?

CHAPTER TEN

PETER GRAVES, a little better but still puffy-faced, came to do the round next morning, after which Kate, feeling sorry for him, asked Zelda to bring him a not-too-hot cup of coffee. As he drank it—gingerly—she asked him how Jean was, for she knew the two were in touch.

'Well, it's early days yet,' he replied, refusing a biscuit, 'but she's been started on intensive physiotherapy, says she's a whizz on crutches, but even so, it looks as though it's going to be a long job. If I hadn't hatched this flaming abscess I'd have driven to Ruislip to see her this weekend.'

He was obviously keen on her, Kate thought, watching his face. Perhaps, when Jean eventually got back they would share the flat over Lew's. Peter, she knew, was at present sharing a house with five other medics. They were probably crowded and the flat would be just right for two people in love. Lucas sprang into her mind at that point, as he was so often wont to do. 'I suppose,' she enquired carefully, 'Lucas is operating this morning?'

'Yep.' Peter finished drinking. 'There was a complicated thoracic injury case brought in an hour ago…a student from Charterhouse, a hit-and-run accident.'

'How awful!' Kate took his cup, after which he went off. Seconds later Chloe rang to say she was feeling better. 'No, it wasn't, nothing like flu, I'll be in at half-twelve.'

And thank heaven for that, Kate thought, with her
eye on Irene Arley who was making her way to the
day-room with Nurse Johnson. She was using her long
white stick, clearing the way in front of anything or
anyone likely to impede her progress. She would probably be discharged next week, which would mean, as
Kate well knew, a certain loss of lynchpin liaison with
Lucas. Irene, without knowing it, she thought, had
helped to thrust Lucas and herself together in that she
had been able to help him learn signing and he had
really applied himself. She smiled a little, remembering
how her mother had exhorted him to practise like mad,
that Saturday in Cletford just on two weeks ago.

Exhorting herself now to get a move on, Kate left
the office, waving to Daphne Harding, who was being
escorted to the bathrooms. There followed the usual
hectic morning of welcoming in new patients, talking
to the social worker who was anxious about the discharge of a frail patient who lived alone. The hospital
chaplain, who was taking a service in the day-room on
Sunday, wanted to consult her about hymns, the phar-
macist reminded her that the three-monthly check on
ward drugs hadn't been done, there was an enquiry
about Christmas trees—how many did the ward
want?—whilst the laundry manager appeared in a great
fury, complaining about bags again. After answering
the phone at least ten times, and setting May Boughton
on staff lunches, Kate went upstairs to her own lunch,
returning to find Chloe in the office, looking her usual
blooming self.

'So, are you really recovered?' Kate enquired.

'Never better.' Chloe beamed.

'Well, you've made a very quick turn-around. We
all thought you were in for flu!'

'Wrong, then!' Chloe pulled Kate in and shut the office door. 'I'm pregnant,' she announced, 'after all these years! I'm due in mid-May, so my doctor told me this morning!'

'Chloe!' Kate gaped, she couldn't help it.

'Well, don't look so surprised. I'm in my forties, not fifties, so I shan't make medical history!' Chloe blew her nose. 'It'll be OK for me to work for another six weeks. I'm seeing the SNO today. I mean to leave, you see—for good, I mean—start a new career at home!'

'Leave nursing altogether?' Kate gaped again.

'Yes. I expect the post will be advertised any time now.' Chloe glanced up at Kate. 'Good chance for you, or Jean, come to that.'

'Not for me. I like the freedom of agency work. I may decide to go back to London,' Kate said with a little slide of panic, knowing that she wouldn't want to be within sight and sound of Lucas if nothing could *ever*—her nails bit into her palms—happen between them.

Expecting him to come on to the ward to see the new patients, she was surprised to see Peter again. 'They lost a patient during surgery this morning,' he told Kate in the office. By 'they' she knew he meant Andrew Chance and Lucas. 'Oh, how awful. You mean the thoracic injury boy?'

'Yes, afraid so. He went into ventricular fibrillation midway through and they couldn't resuscitate him. Only twenty-two. Lucas is seeing his parents right now, they came in from Lincolnshire.'

'What a shock for them.' And how terrible for Lucas, Kate couldn't help thinking.

'It was a hit-and-run case, no witnesses. No one found him for some time, he'd probably lost a heck of

a lot of blood before he ever got to us. Anyway…'
Peter glanced through the viewing window into the
ward '…where's Sister? I thought you told me she was
due back today?'

'She is back, but down seeing the SNO at the moment,' Kate told him with her eye on Walter Harridew
making his thumping way into side-ward one. She had
already briefed Chloe about him, and fervently hoped
that she'd be back to deal with him, should he decide
to erupt again.

She was, and did. 'But I could have done without
him in my condition,' she said, beaming happily at
Kate as she drank her cup of tea.

It was good to be going off shift promptly, Kate was
thinking, when at a little before five p.m. she squeezed
into a lift crowded with a mixture of staff and home-
going visitors. In no way did she expect to see Lucas,
for this wasn't one of his times, but as they reached
the ground floor she found herself looking out for him,
just in case he should appear. He presently did—from
one of the other lifts. Her first impulse was to get as
near to him as possible so that he couldn't fail to see
her, but something held her back, as well as the crowd,
for following close behind him were Fergus Lord and
Claire.

They were hurrying along, trying to talk, or at any
rate Fergus was. Claire had slipped a hand within
Lucas's arm, but withdrew it to button the top of her
coat as they reached the exit doors. Once outside they
were lost to sight and Kate made herself move, walking
slowly so as not to catch up with them. Perhaps they
were talking about the house, the one Fergus had mentioned last night? The thought passed through her
mind, then she gasped as she felt a hand on her arm.

Turning, she saw Clive, and gasped again. What was he doing here? This was Friday and he and Marcus Brandt drove back to town on Fridays. 'Clive, why…?' she started to say, then he tightened his grip on her arm.

'Thought I'd never find you.' He sounded breathless. 'I've got the car over there, tell you everything once we've moved off, I'm on double yellow lines!'

They crossed the forecourt at a run. Clive seemed very disturbed. Perhaps something had happened to Mr Brandt, or perhaps something had gone wrong at the audit. Kate's thoughts ran amok. Clive was usually so calm and composed. What had upset him like this?

'Whatever's happened?' she burst out in alarm.

'In a minute. Let me just get pulled round here.' He reversed into a slip road at the side of the hospital, and switched the engine off. 'There's been a fire at my digs.' He loosened his seat belt, turning round to face her.

'What?'

'Yes, quite bad, too. I went there to fetch the car to drive up to London, arriving just in time to see the fire engine leaving, the police at the gate and old Mrs Boon in next door's garden, sitting on a chair.'

'Was she hurt? Was she taken to hospital? Oh, Clive!' Kate was horrified.

'No, she didn't even inhale much smoke. She was upstairs when it started, smelt burning, had the sense to get out. Her neighbour, a Mrs Potter, rang for help. It started in the kitchen, and as my rooms were over the top, my stuff had to be got out. The police let me go in, and from what I could glean from them the place isn't likely to be habitable for a week or ten days. The electricity's been affected, the fire took a very quick hold.'

'Thank goodness no one was hurt, but how did it start?'

'Mrs B. left the cooker on—one of the boiling rings. I suppose something blew on to that, and she has no smoke alarm, would you believe? Some people never learn.'

'What will she do? Where will she go? Where will *you* go?'

'She's going to stay with Mrs Potter, and I've been offered a bed and breakfast arrangement there, which is very good of her, bearing in mind the lack of notice!' Clive gave a puffing laugh. 'Even so, it's not ideal so far as I'm concerned. I had two rooms at Mrs Boon's— one a small sitting room. Next door I'll have a tiny bedroom only, and after breakfast each day I'll be expected to be absent until it's time to go to bed.'

'Oh, *Lord*!'

'Lunch is no problem, I have that out anyway,' Clive went on, his gloved hand hitting the steering-wheel with an impatient little thump. 'It's just that after five-thirty I'll be adrift in the town.'

Kate stared through the windscreen at the light-beaming traffic passing at the top of the road, then heard herself say, 'How would it be if you came to the flat each evening after work? I'd be bound to be home before you, unless I was on late duty, and we could eat there, or go out sometimes, whatever we liked.'

She had known what his answer would be, of course, even before he leaned sideways, gave her a hug and called her a star. She had known he'd accept, for that was why he'd waylaid her like this. He had hoped, banked on her offering him a haven, had known she would come to his aid. Not that she held this against him, for it was really rather nice to be turned to in a crisis. That's what friends were for.

Even so, as he drove her home before journeying up to London, she had one or two misgivings. Did she really want all her evenings spoken for over the next week or ten days? She couldn't really tip him out before ten or half past, which would leave no time to herself. Also, supposing Lucas called—not that that was likely—or supposing Clive read too much into her wish to help? She had to stop worrying, she told herself later, wondering what to have for supper. At least Clive would take over the culinary side once he was ensconced. He was a super cook, taking time and trouble... For goodness' sake, she'd got it made!

It was Tuesday, though, before they were to eat together in the flat, for on Clive's return from London on Sunday night, he had gone straight to Mrs Potter's, as he had eaten *en route*. On Monday they had dined at the River Lawns Hotel with Marcus Brandt and his formidable cousin—the latter having expressed surprise at Mrs Potter not offering Clive full board. 'I know her slightly, her house is commodious and she's well used to catering. She occasionally takes students in.'

'Well, with Mrs Boon staying there, I expect she felt she'd got enough,' Clive had said, eyes downcast as he'd taken a bone from his fish.

'Even so...'

'Now, Myra, leave it.' Marcus had twinkled at Kate. 'I'm quite sure Clive is happy with the arrangement he's got.'

All this was passing through Kate's mind as she walked to the hospital on Thursday, very nearly a week since the outbreak of the fire. Tomorrow Clive would be going up to London for his usual two nights away and, depending on how the repair work was going on at Mrs Boon's, tonight might just be the last time he'd be eating at the flat. She was a little ashamed of feeling light-hearted at the thought, for Clive had leaned over backwards to help her with the chores, but he was a little exacting. Everything had to be just right. There was no cutting corners with Clive, but that was his nature, of course. Tonight he was cooking the meal as, due to Nurse Liu being ill, she herself would be working till seven, so the day would be long. She sighed as she entered the lift and was taken up to Guthrie Ward.

As she went round distributing the patients' mail—one of her favourite jobs—she reflected that it wouldn't be all that long now before the Christmas trees would be arriving, piled high on long-tailed lorries, honking into the forecourt. Being here at the festive season would be great, she thought. Maybe, just maybe this was where she ought to put down roots.

'I shall miss all the fun, won't I?' Daphne Harding said, as Kate helped her dress. She was going home at noon, her husband was picking her up. She was well now, and discomfort-free, but would need twice-daily baths at home for some weeks, and Kate reminded her of this.

'Yes, I know I've got to do that, to keep me nethers in good order!' she said, pulling a face. 'We'll have a big gas bill for hot water, too, not that my husband will make a fuss. He's a good man is my Bert! Ooh, look.' She broke off suddenly, jerking her jumper down. 'There's Mr Heartthrob, and he's coming this way!'

Kate's own heart did a little flip at the news. She'd only seen Lucas in passing for three days, for Chloe had been on duty to do the honours, but now it was her turn. Trying to conceal too much pleasure she turned to greet him, but Daphne got in first. 'Come to say goodbye to me, Doctor? Thought you would!' Shiny-faced, she grinned up at him. 'I'm your favourite patient, I know!'

'Of course you are, Mrs Harding.' He smiled back at her. 'But now I hope you're all set to go, because your husband is sitting out in the corridor. There he is, look, at the doors!' He wrote 'Discharged' and the date on the notes Kate handed him, then beckoned to Daphne's Bert—a handsome little man, carrying a case, looking a shade self-conscious. Lucas wanted a word with him, and Kate left them to it, going over to the ward desk where Nurse Liu was talking to Ruth Vines—Irene's sister—for Irene, also, was ready to go home, and was sitting on her bed, waiting for someone to tell her that the moment had come.

It was to her that Lucas went next, accompanied by Ruth and Kate. He had his copy of the deaf-blind manual with him. Kate could see it sticking out of the pocket of his white coat. He still wasn't sure of himself without it, and she found this endearing. He was in no sense a know-all, he was big enough to doubt himself in some situations, he never blustered or feigned knowledge of something new to him.

Sitting sideways on the bed and taking Irene's hand, he signed on it, 'This is the big day, Irene.'

'I know it!' Her reply came hoarsely.

'You've done remarkably well.'

Ruth broke in then to say how grateful she was for all that had been done for her sister. 'I'd like to take this opportunity of thanking you, Mr Brown.'

'Well, it's good of you to say so, but we work as a

team, and your sister played her part, doing everything we asked.'

'I have a feeling,' Irene said, 'that you're all sitting there talking about me. I have a sixth sense about these things!' This was said with a laugh as she put out her hand ready to be written on again.

'We plead guilty,' Lucas signed. 'I was just telling your sister how co-operative you've been.' He was having a certain amount of difficulty now—Kate noticed him consulting his leaflet—but he evidently got his point over because Irene answered quickly enough.

'You're kind to say so,' she said, 'but I must have been a pain at times, and for you and Kate to have learned to speak to me has meant so much, especially when—as Ruth has told me—you're always so busy.'

'Believe me, we shall miss you.' Taking Lucas's place, Kate signed on Irene's hand.

'And I you.' There was a distinct tremor in Irene's voice as Kate helped her into a wheelchair. Lucas shook her hand and Kate wheeled her out to the lifts. Irene had wanted to walk, and could have done so, but the corridor was long and full of bustle at this time of day, and in any case Kate had wanted to do this very last thing for her.

Lucas was in the office, signing prescriptions, when she returned. She suggested coffee, but he shook his head. 'No time,' he said, without looking up. 'I'm running late as it is.' He straightened up and moved back from the desk so that Kate could pass. Then, screwing the top on his pen, he mentioned Chloe's pregnancy and her intention to leave nursing. 'Chance for you.' He looked at her keenly. 'Why don't you apply—for her job, I mean? You're in the right grade bracket and you've proved you can manage a ward.'

Kate was flattered. Praise from Lucas meant so very much. 'Thanks for the vote of confidence.' She tried not to look too pleased. 'But that kind of permanent commitment isn't for me.'

'You're not ambitious, then?' And now his voice was implying criticism, not unnoticed by Kate, who felt she should try to justify herself.

'No, I don't think I am,' she said. 'I like to do a good job, but I don't want to be top of the tree. I'm enjoying being here very much indeed, but as soon as Jean comes back I shall leave, as arranged.'

'And just go about doing agency work?' he sounded incredulous.

'Possibly.' His attitude stiffened her even more.

'In Seftonbridge?'

'I'm not sure yet.' She reached up to shut the window, then turned round to face him, very nearly at eye level. 'On the other hand,' she said, irked by the disparagement and criticism he was plainly showing, 'I may go back to London and work there!'

His mouth formed an O then straightened out to emit, 'I see.' He kept it open as though there was more to come, perhaps of a sarcastic nature, but a coughing sound at the open doorway made him swing round to see a hovering Walter Harridew, who had come to take his wife home.

Lucas joined him in the corridor, warning him about allowing Carmen to lift heavy weights. 'Nothing heavier than a frying-pan for several weeks, Mr Harridew!' His attempt at a joke fell flat.

However, all Mr Harridew said in a reminding, blaming kind of way, was, 'And no coughing either, I sincerely hope!'

'*Should* Carmen cough, which she's not doing now,'

Lucas injected smoothly, 'she should gently support her abdomen until the paroxysm has passed. She knows how to do this, both Sister and Nurse Maybury here will have taken her through it all. Now, I'd like to say goodbye to her. Ah, here she is.' He smiled as Carmen appeared in front of them, warmly wrapped in a well-padded puffer coat.

'Looks like she's going to Antarctica,' Walter grumbled, going forward to take her arm and kiss her cheek, and even looking pleased to see her! Wonders never cease, thought Kate, watching their combined rotund shapes ambling up the corridor, flanked by Lucas who presently returned to tell her that Walter had decided not to sue after all.

'He doesn't think he's got enough grounds.'

'Which he hasn't, of course,' Kate said politely but with a certain amount of reserve. She hadn't quite forgiven Lucas for his remarks about her wish to continue to do agency work. Interrupted at this point by her phone ringing…it never seemed to stop…he looked at his watch, mouthed a goodbye and sped off to the men's ward.

Chloe came on duty at noon and Kate went to early lunch, first going down to the hospital shop to buy a newspaper. Lucas was there, doing the same thing, talking to the girl behind the counter, who was staring at him in a star-struck fashion as she handed him his change. Did he, Kate wondered, also gazing, at his delectable rear view, know what an effect he had on that poor bemused girl?

Pocketing his change, he turned and saw her, and for a second looked disconcerted before he said in a breathy voice, 'Hello, it's not very often we meet down here!'

'That's true!' Clearly the more composed of the two, Kate moved past him to get to the counter, aware of him waiting whilst she bought her paper and magazine.

'Plainly it's a case of two great minds thinking alike,' he commented, as they emerged from the shop and stood together in the thin sunshine, neither making any move to part. 'We even read the same paper.' He slapped his against his thigh. 'Must indicate something meaningful, don't you think?'

'I can't think what!' Kate smiled, falling in with his mood, which she felt was purposely friendly to offset his earlier comments about her ambitions. He'd been rude, but in her experience men seldom apologised, just varnished over things with a dollop of charm. Even so, as he stood there in front of her, shading his eyes from the sun, she had the feeling that he was about to say something further and less flippant when he was hailed by Andrew Chance, who was beckoning from the steps.

'Looks like I'm wanted!'

'In demand again!' Now Kate herself was being flippant, and on that note they parted, he swiftly with agile ease, his shadow black and flitting, cleaving the ground at his side.

'I went round to see Mrs Boon at lunchtime,' Clive said when she got home that evening. He was in the kitchen, heating soup, and its spicy scent filled the flat.

'Oh, how are things?' Kate tried not to sound too eager.

'Well, so-so.' He tucked the teatowel he was wearing more securely into the waistband of his trousers. 'The kitchen's safe now, but is being redecorated. What she suggests is that I don't move back in until Wednesday, which means three more evenings with

you, if that's all right. I'll be off to London tomorrow
for the weekend, as usual.'

'OK,' Kate agreed, but only after a pause, which
wasn't lost on Clive.

'We've managed all right so far, haven't we?' He
turned round from the stove. 'And you'll be going
home for the weekend, I expect?'

'Not,' she said, 'till Saturday night. Sunday and
Monday are my days off this week.'

'I'm still hoping that one weekend you'll come up
to London with me. It would redress the balance a little
between us, and if you didn't want to stay at the flat,
one of your old nursing colleagues would surely put
you up. We could visit all our favourite places. It'd be
like old times.'

'Clive, we've had this conversation before,' she
called out from the bedroom, where she was taking off
her coat.

'And you said no. Is it still no?' His voice was a
little sharp in query.

'Yes, I'm afraid it is. I've enjoyed…am enjoying
your company down here. Let's just leave it at that.
You're welcome to stay until Wednesday,' she added,
coming through to unfold the table in the living room
and spread it with a cloth. Before Clive had come she
had eaten off a tray, but he was a man who liked things
more civilised, so for the past week table and cloth had
seen the light of day.

They were halfway through their soup, neither saying very much, when the street doorbell pealed, startling them both.

'Who on earth…?'

'Must be Lew!' Kate literally leapt off her chair. It
might be Lucas, she was sure it was Lucas, and flew

down the stairs. She was right, there he stood in the splash of light from Lew's shop, her fruit and veg box clamped to his front, a bunch of yellow and mauve freesias draped across its top. 'Saw this in the shop, so I told Lew I'd get it to you,' he said. 'And the flowers—slide them off the top, will you?—are from me with apologies for being so rude and crass about your job plans.'

'Oh, Lucas, you shouldn't have!' The trite words shot out of her, making them both laugh.

'Well, aren't you going to let me in…bring this up?'

'Yes, of course. Sorry!' She moved to one side. Why, oh, why couldn't she have been on her own, she thought as they mounted the stairs, Lucas going first.

'I can see you follow the golden rule about eating five portions of fruit and veg every single day!' He pretended to puff and groan with the weight of the box.

A feverish Kate was just about to explain that she was buying for two when Clive appeared at the head of the stairs, still with the teatowel draped round his waist, legs slightly apart. 'What's this, then, a special delivery?' he joked, standing back to let Lucas pass when in the brighter light of the sitting room the two men recognised one another.

Lucas jarred to a halt, almost dropping the box. 'Oh, good Lord.' He swung round to Kate. 'You've got a guest, and I've interrupted your meal!' He could see the laid table, the half-empty soup bowls, the crumble of rolls on their plates.

'No problem.' It was Clive who answered, holding out his arms for the box. 'And as it happens I'm not a guest, I'm here each night. There was a fire at my digs last week and Kate took me in.'

'A *fire*. Was anyone hurt?' Lucas watched Kate remove his flowers from the top of the box before Clive took it into the kitchen.

'Fortunately, no.' Clive's voice floated back to them. 'It happened during the day, so I was at work. My landlady fled to a neighbour.'

'Fortunate that Kate could come to your aid,' Lucas said quietly.

'We tend to be there for one another. Kate and I go back a long way.' Clive returned to the sitting room minus his apron, making a rather obvious play of gathering up the half-empty soup bowls. Kate, aware of an uncomfortable atmosphere snaking about the room, thanked Lucas for the flowers all over again.

'My pleasure,' he said. 'Now I'll leave you in peace.' He turned towards the door in a purposeful manner, but not a quick one. It was plain that he didn't intend to be rushed out by a hostile Clive, who was standing akimbo again. 'I hear you're a first-class skater,' he remarked at the door. 'Claire was full of praise for your skills.'

His mention of Claire was a stab to the heart and Kate drew a shaky breath. Clive, meanwhile, was crossing the room to stand at her side. 'I enjoy the exercise,' he said, 'and it refreshes me mentally, too. Kate and I go to the rink most nights but so far we've not seen you.'

'I go when I can,' Lucas said shortly, 'but my hours don't always suit. When I'm on call I prefer not to venture too far from base.'

'A blood-and-guts job wouldn't suit me.' Clive gave a little laugh that was less than mirthful, more contemptuous, very nearly sneering, in fact.

Kate gasped.

'Well, each to his own,' Lucas said equably. 'As

they say, one man's meat is another man's poison, and a nine-to-five pen-pushing job wouldn't appeal to me.'

Clive was silenced, but only momentarily, for as Lucas stepped out of the flat he remarked, practically on his heels, 'You know, it's odd how things turn out. When we first met it was me turning up here with flowers, feeling that I'd chosen the wrong moment to barge in. Now, tonight, our roles are reversed!'

'*Clive*...for goodness' sake!' Kate was appalled.

Lucas turned slowly round. 'A nod,' he said unsmilingly, 'is as good as a wink, I'm told!' And with that he stepped out onto the landing, closing the door behind him with the kind of click that effectively prevented Kate from rushing out after him.

She swung round to Clive. 'That was so *rude*!'

'I know, and I'm sorry. I shouldn't have said that.' He sank down on a chair. He was pale and his hands were shaking but, then, so were Kate's.

'It's a bit late for apologies.'

They could hear Lucas's car pulling away outside.

'But fancy coming at this time and making the box an excuse. I thought Lew closed at half-five!' Outrage tinged Clive's voice.

'He keeps open till eight on Thursdays, and Lucas was simply trying to help.'

'Trying to help *you* maybe. When I heard the two of you come laughing up the stairs I felt sidelined, pushed out. I knew you didn't want me here.'

'That's not true!' But it was, it was, and Kate knew it. 'You're just imagining things.'

'I don't think so. There's something between you. I've thought so right from the first and tonight, seeing you together, your face all alight...' He moved to the table and stood there, his hands gripping its edge.

'You've never looked like that for me, Kate, not even in our early days!'

'Clive, what's all this about?' Kate asked cautiously.

'Isn't it obvious?' He inclined towards her. 'I still have feelings for you. No, hear me out,' he said sharply, as she made to speak. 'Marcus was right, I did pull strings to get sent on this audit. I meant to get into contact with you, was going to ring you up. Then we met at the hotel and I couldn't believe my luck, especially when you agreed—fairly readily—to see me again. It was obvious that we still had a lot in common and I could feel you warming towards me, especially when you offered help after the fire. Oh, I know it's not like it used to be, we'll never get that back, but I care for you and I'd like us to try again. Perhaps we could even think about marriage after a time. With my job at the stage it is, I ought to settle down…'

'That sounds awfully like a business arrangement,' Kate said when she could speak.

'Well, in a sense I suppose it is. Marcus says—'

'Oh, damn Marcus!' she exploded. 'I'm not a chattel, Clive. I'd never marry any man just to settle him, quite the reverse! I know I should be flattered by what you've just said, but I'm not, I'm outraged!'

'It's *him*, isn't it?' Clive had his back to her now, and she was able to stall on that one and arrange her face.

'I'm fond of you, Clive, and I'm sorry all this has blown up,' she qualified. 'I've enjoyed your company this fortnight…'

'But now you want me to go. That's it, isn't it? You want to be shot of me.'

'I think that might be best, yes.' She was ashamed

of the relief that spread over her as she said the words—anything for this scene to end.

He went very quickly, collecting his jacket and picking up his boots from the landing. 'Bye,' he said. 'I shan't trouble you again.'

There followed an awkward pause, broken by Kate who managed to say, 'Please, drive carefully.'

Clive went swiftly down the stairs and round to the yard to get his car.

CHAPTER ELEVEN

KATE found herself unable to mention the scene in the flat when she met Lucas in the car park the following morning. A kind of perverse loyalty to Clive stopped her apologising for him. Anyway, Lucas had been pretty rude, too, calling him a pen-pushing type.

She waited for him, though, as, slightly ahead of her, he got out of his car.

'Hello. So you've driven in this morning.' He greeted her affably enough.

'Only because it's raining,' she said, as indeed it was—heavy, splashing-up-from-the-pavement kind of rain—which might have been why he didn't fall into step beside her but hurried by, head bent.

He was on the ward early, before Chloe had had time to do the report. He wanted to speak to Mrs Lamb, who had been admitted the day before with a troublesome stone blocking one of her salivary glands, making eating painful. There was also, Kate noticed, a child in bed six, a little girl of around ten years old, with whom Lucas had a brief word. 'He wants the list changed,' Chloe said when he'd gone. 'Mrs Lamb is to go down at ten, the gastrectomy, Miss Severs, has been moved to this afternoon. You can prep Mrs Lamb at nine.'

'Why have we got a child on the ward?' Kate was asking, when Lucas, coming back to retrieve his pen which he'd left on the desk, overheard her, and cut in on Chloe's reply.

'Because Paediatrics is full and because all the child

needs is a pacemaker inserted into her chest by the registrar, Clement Byers. She's not, therefore, my patient. I doubt if she'll be in here more than two days, so why the harassed expression, Kate? Don't you like nursing children?' The question, sharply voiced, came out as an attack.

Kate rose up to defend herself. 'As a matter of fact, yes, I do enjoy it. I happen to like children, and I'm sorry if I sounded curt. I didn't mean it.'

'I'm glad to hear it!' Off he went again, and Chloe puffed out her cheeks.

'What's rattled his cage?' she said. 'Not that I care. Being pregnant has put me on a higher plane. I transcend all petty irritations. You should try it some time, Kate!'

Lucas didn't reappear, and on Saturday Kate knew she wouldn't see him for, unless he was on call or there was some dire emergency, his weekends were spent at home. As she drove home herself on Saturday evening, she wondered if he'd be riding on Sunday, as she hoped to do. To meet him then, to meet him at the stables, would be a good time to straighten things out. Naturally she wouldn't tell him about Clive's outburst, but she could make it plain to him that Clive hadn't been staying with her in the way that he'd inferred. She refused to question why she felt it necessary to clear the air with Lucas—refused, for one second, to acknowledge the fact that she was falling in love with him.

Knowing her mother's fondness for Clive, she didn't want to tell her about Thursday night's debacle, or that she wasn't seeing him again. However, the subject wasn't to be avoided for during their pre-supper drink, Paula asked how he was, and whether they'd been out very much. She also asked how he was finding his digs. 'I know what a fusspot he is.'

So it all came out, Paula drinking and listening without saying a word, till Kate ground to a halt.

Paula took her time replying, then ultimately said, 'It would have been better if you hadn't taken up with him again.'

Full to the brim with remorse, not regret, Kate looked back at her. 'Don't you think I don't know that, Mother? I've been feeling bad about it ever since, but at least—' she hardened her heart '—it's all straightened out now. Clive will have to look elsewhere for a likely "suit-his-job" wife. He'll have to leave me out of his calculations, because that's what they were.'

Wisely Paula said no more and, after a second glass of wine each, reasonable mother and daughter relations were resumed, Paula asking if Kate was riding next day. 'Yes, I hope to, in the morning,' she replied, 'unless you've anything else arranged.'

'Well, I'm decorating the spare room. I thought you might help, in the afternoon, not the morning. You're so much better at it than me. We could strip the walls and do the painting tomorrow, then, if you liked, you could start the paper-hanging on Monday when I'm at work. Decorating,' Paula added, getting up to put the potatoes on to boil, 'is good for the soul.'

Seeing Lucas would be good for the soul, too, Kate thought ruefully, but he wasn't at the stables next day. Hercules was hanging his handsome head over his door as she entered the yard. She went over to speak to him and he whinnied gently, blowing down his nose. His ears were well forward, indicating good humour, and she stroked his nose, liking the feel of him under her hand. 'Are you going out this morning, then? Is that what you want?' she crooned.

'Mr Vernon will be taking him later on.' Iris had come up behind her. 'Mr Brown had him out yesterday, he's not coming in today.' She had Cascade with her, tacked up and ready for Kate to mount, which she did, wasting no more time, turning the little mare towards Loamers Lane and the open heath, aware of the flat feeling of dejection that disappointment brought.

All in all, though, as the ride took hold, as the familiar movements of the horse beneath her impinged on her consciousness, she was able to take pleasure in the sparkling December morning, in the waved greetings from other riders, even in the sound of Cletford's church bells coming up from the town. Men, she was thinking as she handed Cascade over to Iris an hour later, men, who needs them? There are other joys in the world.

Next day, however, as she set about her task in the spare bedroom, as she measured and cut and pressed soggy paper on to the walls, her thoughts kept straying to Clive. Her mother had been right. It *would* have been better not to have seen him after their chance meeting at the hotel. He wouldn't have liked it, but he wouldn't have been hurt or especially surprised, because he wasn't vain. He wasn't one of those men who thought they were God's gift to women. 'I've made a right mess of things,' she said out loud. 'Not that there's anything I can do about it now. Best to leave well alone.'

She continued working until one o'clock, when she ate a bacon sandwich, and relished every crumb. By six o'clock, when her mother got in, the spare room was in its new dress, its window cleaned, carpet vacuumed, radiator turned back on. Paula, who'd been worried about Kate all day, was lavish in her praise.

'It's fantastic!' she said, giving her daughter a hug.

It was nine p.m., their supper long done, when they heard Kate's mobile ring from the pocket of her overcoat in the hall. Not many people knew her number—only Clive and the hospital. She sped to answer it, not unduly alarmed, more surprised than anything, but alarm shot through her in a stab as Claire announced herself.

'Claire... Good heavens. What...?'

'There's been an incident at the ice rink involving your Clive. I was there and saw it. He was attacked by an onlooker and brought here to Casualty. He's unconscious. I think you should come!'

'Attacked on the rink? But why...? Whatever...?'

'Just come,' Claire urged.

'Well, of course I'll come, but I'm at Cletford, so I'll be twenty minutes or so!' Still not convinced that Claire wasn't exaggerating, being her usual bossy self, Kate hurried upstairs to fetch her coat and bag, telling her mother what had happened.

'Good Lord, is it serious?' Paula came out to the garage with her.

'Pretty nasty for Clive, I should imagine, but I doubt if it's serious.'

Serious enough for him to be taken to hospital, Kate thought as she drove swiftly along the Seftonbridge Road, reaching the hospital and the entrance to A and E in fifteen minutes flat.

Claire was waiting by the reception desk, easy to pick out from the crowd in her scarlet skating outfit. When she saw Kate she raised an arm and stayed where she was till Kate joined her. 'Before you ask, he's been sent up to Neuro. Lucas managed to get him a bed and arranged for a scan, which he's probably had by now!'

'To Neuro? A scan?' Real alarm now prickled Kate's skin. 'What happened to him? How was he hurt?'

'He was hit in the face as he was coming off the ice. He'd been doing stunts, drawing a lot of attention. This guy started calling him names, shouting obscenities and using his fists. Clive, still with his skates on, couldn't save himself and he went down, striking the back of his head on the edging near the seats. I was nearest to him. Someone called an ambulance, and I came in here with him.'

'Did Lucas examine him? How bad is he?'

'Well, he's concussed, obviously.' For a second the old scornful note was back in Claire's voice. 'Anyway, here's Lucas now, you can ask him yourself. I've got to go. I've left my car at the rink, I don't want it stolen!'

'Thank you for ringing me, and for bringing him here,' Kate remembered to say, before pushing her way through the queue at the desk and joining Lucas.

'Oh, good, you've made it.' His hand clamped her shoulder.

'How is he? You've seen him, haven't you? I want to know how he is,' Kate shouted above the babble of sound that was part and parcel of A and E at this time of night.

'Yes, I saw him. I'm on call till midnight. The good news is that he has no tissue damage or skeletal injuries, but he's concussed, not responsive to stimulae and he has a slow pulse and low BP. On these findings I sent him straight up to Neuro for a scan, which he should have had by now.'

'Can I go up there to see him?'

'I don't know about seeing him, but we'll go up and find out.' Lucas was being kind but very, very professional. So this, Kate thought, was what it was like to be treated as an anxious visitor—this was the receiving end.

'Clive is so unaggressive, why would anyone attack him?' she burst out in the lift.

'Must have been some sort of nutter, there are always those about. Claire didn't say if anyone nabbed him, but let's hope they did. Here we are now.' The lift settled itself, its doors swept back and as they stepped out of it Kate was aware of unfamiliar surroundings, of an almost uncanny hush, dimmed lighting and lack of bustle—night-time on Neuro Ward.

They went to Sister's office, where Charles Rye—a clean-shaven man of about Lucas's age—was talking with a senior nurse. Lucas introduced Kate, saying that she was a nurse on the surgical unit. 'She's also, as I told you, a friend of Clive Mantel's.'

'What did the scan show? Can I see him? I'd like to see him, please.' Kate was trying to sound assertive, but failing miserably.

Charles looked at her with interest, seeing before him an anxious-eyed young woman, looking about eighteen, with hair the same colour as his wife's straying over her shoulders, paint-daubed jeans emerging from the hem of her navy coat.

'The scan,' he said gently, drawing a chair forward for her, 'shows no fracture of skull, so there's no need for surgical intervention. There's no sign, so far, of haemorrhage, but there's considerable swelling—oedema, in other words—which we're trying to keep under control, but as a nurse you'll know that dramatic changes can occur very suddenly in head injury patients. We've got him in one of our side-wards and, yes, of course you can see him, but first of all Staff Nurse Kyle here would like the usual admission details, names of any relatives we should contact and his next of kin.'

'Clive was orphaned as a child and has no close relatives. He was brought up by an aunt who lives in Leicestershire. Mr Brandt, his senior partner, is staying at the River Lawns Hotel, he may know the aunt's telephone number, it could be in the office records,' Kate finished, feeling slightly sick. Surely Clive wasn't going to die.

'We'll ring Mr Brandt. In the meantime, you go in and see the patient.' Charles smiled at her. 'You, too, if you like, Lucas. After all, you saw him first!'

A junior nurse was sitting with Clive, who lay inert, flat on his back with only one pillow, arms outside the coverlet. His face was the colour of putty and clammy, and he was breathing shallowly, making little sighing sounds.

Kate sat on the chair the young nurse had vacated and put a hand on Clive's arm—a bare arm, almost hairless. Clive was wearing a hospital gown. He looked young, vulnerable, unlike himself. Kate's insides churned.

'How do *you* think he is?' She turned round to Lucas, who was standing behind her chair.

'He's a fit man, Kate, with a good physique—' At that moment his pager bleeped. 'It's no good, I'll have to go, but I'll come up later if I can!'

'It's all right.' She nodded, knowing full well that being on call meant just that, but she could have done with his company, his reassurance. She looked at Clive again. Perhaps if she'd been with him this wouldn't have happened. Perhaps if there hadn't been that awful scene in the flat last Thursday, Clive wouldn't be lying here now.

Marcus, almost as shocked as Kate, arrived at half past ten. He looked at the recumbent Clive with horror. 'What a thing to happen!' he choked. But he was businesslike, too, going into the office to give all details they needed then leaving quickly, telling Kate he was going to fetch Clive's car from the rink. 'If I can get a cab quickly, I'll get there before the place closes for the night.'

Kate stayed with Clive. Any minute now he might come round, she told herself. Her vigil was interrupted quarter-hourly by the nurse recording his obs. 'No change,' she'd say to Kate each time. What she'd like to say, Kate knew, was, Why don't you go home and let us do our job in peace? She stayed, though and was still there when the night superintendent came to do her round. She was still there when Charles Rye reappeared, still there when a patient arrested in the main ward and the resuscitation team rushed past in the corridor, still there when Lucas came back.

'For goodness' sake, Kate, it's gone midnight, you're doing no good here!' He pulled no punches. 'You won't be fit to do your job tomorrow, and you know how short-handed we are!'

'I'm on lates tomorrow!' Kate felt glued to the chair.

'Which is less than twelve hours away.' He had her by the elbow and was hoisting her up, and to her surprise, and possibly his, she allowed it to happen, allowed herself to be buttoned into her coat and taken downstairs.

'Are you...' she cleared her dry throat '...off duty

now?' For the first time that evening she had a good look at him, which revealed very little under the overhead lights in the forecourt. His abrupt 'Yes' showed that he was just as tired as she was. She felt a flash of gratitude to him for wresting her away from the sights and sounds of Neuro, yet she still wanted, for some perverse reason, to go flying back up there again. 'I wanted to stay until Clive came round.' Her voice had a thin, tinny sound.

'That could take hours. Meanwhile, I'm running you home.'

'I drove here from Cletford, I've got my own car.' She was set to argue now.

'From Cletford?' He sounded surprised. 'So that's why you weren't at the rink?'

'In a way, yes.' She clapped a hand to her mouth. 'I've forgotten his landlady. I should have let her know, she'll be wondering what's happened to him!'

'I thought he was staying with you at the flat.'

'Only eating with me,' she said, 'in the evenings, due to that business with the fire.' Remembering those times—and some of them had been fun—made her feel that the end of them, the *way* they had ended, was all her fault. She could have been more kind, she could have let him off more gently, not sent him off in a huff.

She was tired and miserable, and not very warm, so she huddled down into her coat. Her eyes filled and overflowed and silent tears rolled down her cheeks and onto her coat. She brushed at them with her hand, turning her face away from Lucas as he guided her to his car.

Princes Parade had little traffic, Bridge Street none at all. There was a full moon, and its eerie light spilled over the two of them as Lucas unlocked her street door. 'I'll ring,' Kate said feverishly, 'early tomorrow, while the night staff are still on. Marcus will want to know how Clive is. He'll want to know what to do about getting someone down to take his place. Clive has a lot of standing in the firm, he's not just a pen-pushing type!'

'I'm quite sure he's not.' Lucas's voice sounded clipped.

'But that's what you called him,' she flashed, wondering why she was fighting Lucas, why she felt so at odds with him.

Their goodnight was brief, but she managed to apologise before going in and closing the door.

Her mother, when she rang her, was unusually comforting. 'Clive's always looked after himself, darling. He's fit, he'll come through this. I'll drive in tomorrow evening, see both you and him.'

Feeling calmer, Kate decided against ringing Mrs Potter, who was elderly and might be asleep. I'll walk round there first thing in the morning, she thought. By then there may be good news. And there was, so far as it went, for when she rang Neuro at seven a.m. Nurse Kyle told her that Clive had regained consciousness at three o'clock. 'He's confused, naturally, didn't know where he was. He's been sleeping on and off since. He may not know you when you come, so don't expect too much.'

'Is he in pain?'

'Headache, which is only to be expected, but we're giving him something for that.'

An hour later, washed and dressed, Kate walked the half-mile to Elvington Road, where a surprised Mrs Potter told her she'd come to the wrong house. 'Mr

Mantel lodges next door with my friend, Mrs Boon,' she said. When Kate, even more surprised than her, mentioned the fire, she was told that although it had been very frightening at the time, very little damage had been done and Mr Mantel had been able to resume living there when he returned from his weekend in London.

Mrs Boon, whom Kate went to next, confirmed all this, adding that Clive had gone onto a bed and breakfast basis after the fire. 'But that was his choice, not mine, Miss Maybury. Quite frankly, I couldn't understand it. There was scant damage to my kitchen, everything was in good order. As for him not coming home last night, I assumed he was with a friend. Naturally I'm sorry about what's happened, very sorry indeed. Even so, I would like to know, in due course, if and when he'll be coming back.'

'Yes, of course,' Kate agreed. 'I'll see that you're told.' She was glad to get away, both to escape from the indignant Mrs Boon and to get her head round the fact that Clive had been—to put it politely—economical with the truth. Not that this really mattered now, all that mattered was him getting well. Even so, no one liked being lied to. It made them look a fool.

She would have forgiven him anything, however, when she saw him half an hour later—confused and rambling, not recognising her, complaining about the light. There was little point in staying with him so, turning, she made to go, then ran into Charles Rye coming out of the main ward.

'Ah, I see we're in nursing mode this morning.' His admiring gaze rested on the soft swell of her breasts beneath the buttoned uniform dress, on the curve of her throat, on her anxious face, on her neatly coiled copper

hair. 'But why the sad face?' He drew her to one side
as a young nurse with a load of sheets made her way
past them. 'Clive's condition this morning is much as
I expected it to be. His pulse rate and BP are coming
up to normal as the brain swelling recedes. The rest-
lessness and slight delirium are to be expected, and
may continue on and off for a time. By this evening I
expect to see a clear improvement. It's early days yet,
you know.'

Kate nodded, still unconvinced, finding it difficult to
relate the incoherent, helpless man on the bed to the
healthy, vigorous one that was Clive. It was a relief to
get down to Guthrie Ward and a sympathetic Chloe,
who'd heard all about his attack from Claire at coffee-
time in the canteen. 'Making herself the heroine of the
house.' Chloe didn't like Claire. 'I bet she'll be up
there this evening, drooling all over him!'

After this little outburst which, in spite of everything, made Kate laugh, Chloe proceeded with the report, bringing Kate up to date with the patient traumas
over the past two days. 'Mrs Lamb—the salivary stone
patient—is still on fluids only. We've got two pre-op
gastrectomies, they're on the list for tomorrow. I've put
them in adjoining beds as they know one another
slightly. They spend most of their time gossiping and
breaking wind! Lucas will be up to see them later, and
I expect that, as usual, he'll arrive in the middle of
visiting or during our quiet hour.'

He came during the tail end of visiting, just as a
toddler—who'd been grizzling on and off all the afternoon—had a full-scale screaming tantrum and had to
be removed, kicking, under the arm of a furious-faced
May Boughton with the young mother trailing behind.
May came back, ill-tempered and battered. 'Bloody

kid,' she said. 'Fancy bringing a two-year-old into a surgical ward!'

'My sentiments exactly, Nurse Boughton.' But Lucas was looking amused as he emerged from the ward with Chloe, whom he proceeded to tease. 'See what's in store for you, Sister!' He winked at Kate who was in the kitchen, searching for extra vases for all the bunches of flowers brought in that afternoon. 'You all right?' he enquired, stopping in the doorway, Chloe having been waylaid by one of the social workers.

'I'm fine.' She smiled, her heart lifting at the sight of him.

'Seen Clive today?'

'Yes, just briefly this morning. He didn't know me, but Mr Rye seems to think... Well, he thinks—' she faltered a little '—that he's going on all right. I'm going up again this evening, during my supper break.'

Lucas came further into the room. 'It's always hard,' he said, 'when a patient is known, and important to you, Kate. A whole new set of feelings come into play then.'

Kate nodded, for he was right, they did, but that wasn't the reason why a lump like a rock blocked her throat, almost choking her as she said, 'I wish I'd been with him last night, then he might not have been attacked!'

'Darling, you can't know that for certain.'

The endearment caught her off guard, and for a second the need to go to him and put her arms round his back, and have him hold her, was so acute and so compelling that she had to turn her back and fiddle with the taps on the big porcelain sink. 'I'd better get on, it's time Chloe went off duty,' she managed to say, hearing him reply but not catching what he said. When she dared to turn round he was gone.

Paula arrived during evening visiting, and she and Kate saw Clive together. This time Kate could see a change in him. He was sitting propped up for a start, and he knew both her and her mother, where he was and why. He was vague, though, about what had happened, and kept asking about his car.

'I get the feeling,' Paula said, as they took the lift to ground level, 'that he's not especially wanting to recall very much. He's happy to exist in his twilit world, just for the time being.'

'He's got retrograde amnesia, Mother. He's not acting up,' Kate defended him, looking at her watch. It was time she was back on her ward. But Lucas was in the foyer with Fergus Lord. Another minute or two wouldn't matter. Any moment now he'd turn round and see them.

Then Paula brought this about by exclaiming in a loud voice, 'There's Lucas Brown!'

Both he and Fergus swung round, Lucas coming forward and shaking hands with Paula. 'Mrs Maybury, good to see you again!' His smile included Kate.

'The last time we met was in the Rutland Arms at Cletford.' Paula took a good look at him. 'You're not like your father, are you? When is he coming back from the health resort place?'

'I'm fetching him at the weekend.' Lucas blinked. Paula Maybury took some getting used to. 'He'll have been away a month this time.'

'Good for him to have a change of scene.' Paula buttoned the top of her coat, shaking her head at Lucas's offer of a lift home. 'Thank you, but, no, I have my own transport, and in any case I'm having supper with friends at River Lawns. Right, then, darling.' She kissed her daughter. 'You'd better get off to your post, and don't forget to let me know how Clive goes on.'

'Of course not.' Kate made for the stairs, watching her voluble mother, flanked by Lucas and the bobbing Fergus Lord, step out onto the forecourt.

CHAPTER TWELVE

ON WEDNESDAY Clive was up for a time, still complaining of a headache and giddiness, but on Thursday he asked to see Claire, to enquire if his attacker had been caught. When she said no, and that he must have got away, he rounded on her peevishly. 'But *why* wasn't he caught, with all those people about? How could he possibly have escaped?'

Kate, who sympathised with him, made soothing noises, but Claire seemed a little agitated. 'He's never once thanked me for all I did,' she complained to Kate out in the corridor.

'Well, he's still trying to get his head round it all,' Kate said, and Lucas, who was also present, backed her up.

'Claire likes heaps of praise,' he said, as the latter took herself off, 'but in a crisis there's no one to beat her for clear-headedness and guts.'

Kate was instantly, furiously jealous, which was so childish she could have kicked herself and mentally did so as she went about her duties—prepping two patients for surgery, checking the drugs cupboard with May and comforting the newly post-op patients, especially the two gastrectomies in adjoining beds who were convinced they were going to die. By the evening, up seeing Clive again, it was still her job to be comforting. He was back in bed, not physically worse but worried and irritable. 'I'd feel better if I had my own clothes.

Spending my time in these hospital night things makes me feel like an invalid.'

'I'll fetch all your belongings. I was going to, anyway—from Mrs Boon's,' she said, laying just the faintest emphasis on the name. Clive didn't react, and when she suggested that she tell Mrs Boon he wouldn't be coming back, he just nodded offhandedly and said that might be best.

'Marcus is coming in later and bringing my stand-in, Celia Bateman, to see me. I know her, of course, she was the one who wanted to come on the audit in the first place.' His eyes met Kate's and then slid away. 'Well, now she's got her wish.'

Coming back with a heavy bag of his clothes on Friday at midday, she was just leaving the car park when she saw Lucas making for his car. 'You coming or going?' He looked at the bag.

'Coming. These are Clive's clothes. He asked for them yesterday.'

'He's doing well, I'm told.' She turned away from him. A strand of her hair had escaped from its bun and was waving about in the wind. When she turned round she was pink-flushed.

'He's not easy to visit,' she said. 'His aunt, his next of kin and virtually only relative, rings every day, but elects not to come, which is pretty hard on him.'

'Well, I'm sure you make all the difference.' He stooped and picked up the bag. 'I'll take this to the lifts for you.'

'But you were just on your way out.' Dear Lucas... dear Lucas... I love you. The words rang and jangled in her head. Oh, if only she could let them out. But he was telling her that he would be away for a few days, fetching his father home from Tring, and moving house.

'How exciting!' Her words sounded flat, even to her own ears.

He looked at her sharply as he set the bag down in the foyer by the lifts. 'Most likely, when I get back, Clive will have been discharged,' he said, 'but at the moment he's bound to be feeling low. Amnesia is very hard to cope with, like moving about in a fog.'

They stood there, he smiling, she feeling desperate, then the lift made its appearance, staff poured out of it and he was raising his hand and mouthing, 'Goodbye.' Pushing the bag forward with her foot, Kate got into the lift.

On the following Wednesday Clive was discharged, but was warned that as his work involved intense mental activity, it would be advisable for him to convalesce at home for three to four weeks. He was aghast at this at first, but told Kate when she went to say goodbye that so long as he was in his own place, with his own things around him, he would make great strides.

'Not literally, I hope, not to the extent of jogging over London Bridge!' Kate said, as she kissed him swiftly, her eye on Marcus at the wheel of his BMW, ready to drive off. Clive seemed to be hesitating and she held her breath. Please, don't let him mention anything about the fire, and the flat, and our argument, or, even worse, suggest that we meet up again, she found herself praying.

He was moving his feet, looking down at the ground. 'It was great to run into one another again, wasn't it?' His voice was a thread of sound.

'It was, it was fun.'

He was moving to the car.

'Safe journey. Take care!'

The car moved off. Marcus waved but Clive was engrossed in fastening his seat belt and didn't look up again.

He remembered all right...remembered *everything* that had happened, Kate felt sure of that, but who could blame him for feigning not to? Who could blame him for existing in the shadows for a little while longer, if that would save his face?

Up on Guthrie Ward excitement abounded, for the Christmas trees had arrived—a six-foot high one for the main ward, a slightly smaller one for the top of the corridor. The baubles to hang on them had arrived, too, and the two junior nurses pleaded to be allowed to wind on the coloured lights. 'Not until they've been tested,' Chloe decreed. It was the quiet hour, and she wasn't best pleased to have Bill from Maintenance rattling paper and scraping about with plugs.

Lucas was in the ward—another fact that didn't please her. 'Why does he have to come at this time?' She pulled Kate into the office for the hand-over report. 'Still, I'll say this for him, he doesn't give himself airs and expect to be waited on. He's come to see the four on his list for tomorrow. Being away for five days hasn't helped, not with Mr Chance being off for the rest of this week.'

Rushed Lucas might be, but his mood was upbeat. 'Christmas,' he said, handing four sets of notes back to Chloe in the office, 'is something I always look forward to—the season of comfort and joy, and all that! How about you?' He swung round to Kate who was going past the door with a pile of sheets.

'On duty, or off, I love it,' she said, meeting his eyes,

returning his smile, and feeling as she did so—in spite
of the sheets—some of that joy already beginning to
spill all over her.

There was no sign of him on Thursday, which didn't
surprise her with the theatre list he had. Peter Graves
came to do the round and Kate accompanied him, but
nothing really out of the way happened till Chloe came
back from early lunch with what she called startling
news.

'Well, come on, then, don't keep me in suspense!'
Kate turned round from closing the office window
against the grey fog outside.

'Claire Jevons has got herself engaged!'

Kate froze as she stood, forcing herself to smile as
she said, 'To Lucas, of course?'

'To *Lucas*? Good heavens, no. That was over ages
ago, if it was ever properly on. Oh, I know she's always
trailing around after him, but that's how she is. No,
she's marrying her cousin Hugh after Christmas and
going to live in New Zealand.'

Kate had to sit down. Claire was engaged to
Hugh...to *Hugh*. And not only that, but she was going
to New Zealand to live! But what about Lucas? How
was he feeling? Would *he* be glad?

Chloe snapped back into working mode. 'You'd better take your lunch-break now,' she said, 'but before
you go, get someone to take that lunch trolley out of
the ward. Fancy leaving it there when it's done its job
a good half-hour ago!'

It wasn't Kate's habit to seek Claire out, but that
evening, coming off shift, she decided to do just that.
Not only was it the done thing to offer congratulations,
but she could truthfully say she was glad. She ran
Claire to ground in one of the cloakrooms on the ortho

floor. Claire was all smiles. 'Were you surprised?' she asked. Kate admitted that she had been, adding—and meaning it—that she thought Hugh was very nice.

'He is,' Claire said, as the two of them left the cloak-room and made for the landing and lifts. 'We're both going to be in the Fox and Hounds at six tomorrow evening. I'm asking one or two people from here to join us for a drink and I'd like you to come as you've met Hugh. I'm asking Lucas and the ortho registrar, and two of the X-ray team. I mentioned it to Chloe, but she says she's on late duty tomorrow. See if you can persuade her to come, though. Surely she can leave one of her minions in charge of the ward for half an hour or so.'

Kate accepted on behalf of herself, and said she'd work on Chloe, but the main thought that filled her mind was that Lucas would be there. She wondered how he really felt about the engagement for, although she wanted to believe Chloe, she found it difficult to believe that there was absolutely nothing left between him and Claire. Whenever she had seen them together Claire had seemed absolutely besotted with him—all ready to go, in fact—and there were few men who didn't and wouldn't take advantage of that.

Chloe reiterated her wish not to go. 'What's the point?' she said. 'I can't drink, not in my condition, and I'd have to leave May in charge here.'

'But not for long, and you can drink juice,' Kate urged. 'I don't want to walk into the pub all on my own. As I'm off shift at half-four, I'll go home and change, then call for you here at six.'

'Oh, all right, if I must,' Chloe sighed, but yielded with good grace.

Just after six the following evening they were part

of the congratulatory group in the Fox and Hounds, raising their glasses to a radiant Claire and Hugh.

Lucas came ten minutes later. 'Got caught up on the phone,' he said, drinking a toast to his hosts then going to sit with Kate. 'Long time no see,' he said.

'Not all that long, surely!' Kate, in a narrow black skirt and vivid multistriped sweater, smiled happily over her glass of champagne—her second glass. She'd better watch it, she thought, or she'd start losing control.

Claire joined them, asking if she'd heard from Jean. '*I* have,' Chloe broke in. 'She rang the ward this morning. She hopes to be back in her flat and working at the end of January.'

'It looks like I'll be leaving then,' Kate said.

'What will you do? Go back to London?' Claire asked, taking the chair on the other side of Lucas.

'I may, yes.' Kate drained her glass. 'But I haven't decided yet.'

'She could do my job on her head. I can't think why she doesn't put in for it.' Chloe got to her feet. 'I must go,' she said. 'Time I was making sure no one's died in my absence!'

'I'll see you back.' Lucas had risen when she had, then one of the ortho nurses, also returning on shift, offered to accompany her.

'Anyone would think being pregnant renders me incapable,' Chloe sniffed, but she accepted just the same and pushed Lucas down in his seat, telling him to enjoy his evening.

'I will.' He grinned. 'But it's tonic only…' he held up his glass '…because I'm driving home afterwards.'

'And by home, Lucas, do you mean your new place?' Hugh had joined them.

'I do, yes,' Lucas replied, 'although I'm not its owner yet, merely a tenant until contracts are exchanged.'

'What about Gervase? Is he sharing it with you?'

'Absolutely not.' Lucas sounded mildly scandalised. 'Dad wouldn't move in even if I wanted him to. Nothing would prise him out of Badgers End, but I'll be able to have him to stay occasionally, give him a change of scene, which I could never do at Maitland House as there wasn't a lift. Anyway, he and I are both agreed that we don't like flats.'

Kate happily and just a shade hazily, yet missing nothing, was listening to the ebb and flow of their talk till she felt Lucas turn to her. 'You're very quiet, Kate.'

'But, then, Kate,' Hugh said, inclining towards her, 'has a restful quality about her. I noticed that on the two occasions she and I met.'

Kate coloured, she could feel her cheeks scorching. Lucas shifted in his chair. Hugh wasn't drunk, but the rich red wine which he preferred to champagne was making him benign.

'Hugh, we ought to be making tracks.' Claire's voice intruded. 'We're going to see that new play at The Arts, and they have an unbreakable rule about not letting anyone in once the curtain has gone up.'

By this time most of the others had taken their leave, muttering about shifts and being on call and reiterating good wishes and thanks.

'You going my way?' Lucas looked at Kate, retrieving her bag from the back of her chair.

'Well I wasn't.' She prevaricated a little, playing her cards just right. 'I'm off for the weekend, and I'd like to go home, but it'll have to be the flat tonight as I've had too much champagne to drive.'

'I'll drive you…simple.' Lucas stepped right into the trap, not that he hadn't—in his abstemious, unalcoholic state—seen it being set up for him. 'I'll fetch the car round, you wait here.'

Kate nodded, her excitement mounting as she made her way to the toilets, where she found Claire renewing her make-up and fluffing out her hair. Their eyes met in the mirror. 'Thanks for asking me tonight,' Kate said, when Claire didn't speak. 'I really enjoyed myself.'

'Good.' Claire moved to one side so that Kate could come to the basin, then said, 'If you're thinking of embarking on an affair with Lucas, remember that's all it will be. He'll promise nothing. The only thing he's committed to is furthering his career. He's ambitious and he doesn't let anything or anyone get in the way of that. I just thought, as you seem to be smitten with him, that you ought to know the score.'

'Thanks for the warning,' Kate managed to say. She even managed to laugh. She was relieved when Claire said nothing more, just opened the door and went out.

Drying her hands, still feeling shaken, Kate reflected on the fact that, even with her future secure with Hugh, Claire couldn't bear the thought of her getting close to Lucas. It's called being dog in the manger, she told herself, with a bit of spite as well. She tried to dismiss it, to shrug it off, but she was very quiet when she got into Lucas's car.

'You sleepy,' he asked her once they were clear of the town, 'or is the champagne wearing off?'

She laughed and told him neither, and warmth invaded the car, settling between and over them, making talk flow easily. She asked him about his house, exactly where it was.

'Midway between here and Cletford, almost exactly,' he replied, passing a bus crammed with passengers.

'Then I'll be taking you three, no, six miles out of your way, counting coming back,' she said.

'I'm in no hurry,' he assured her. She felt him glance at her, felt her pulses racing, her fingertips burning, her whole body alert.

The way lay clear ahead, tall beeches bordering the road, wide grass verges sloping back to low scrawny hedges dividing newly ploughed fields. He was driving slowly as though needing to talk, but it was several minutes before he asked her if she was seriously thinking of nursing in London again.

'Yes, I think you could say I'm considering it,' she said quietly, and she was speaking the truth for if nothing was to happen between her and Lucas, the best thing she could do was get out of range and somehow…somehow put him out of her life.

'To join Clive, I suppose?' The question rapped out of him. 'You still love him, don't you…your faithful, good-looking, pen-pushing friend?'

'You shouldn't say that!'

'Are you in love with him?'

'No, I love you!' And now she was almost shouting the words, and now he was stopping the car, drawing up on the verge, unfastening their seat belts, snatching her up to him.

'How I've longed to hear you say that, my darling, darling Kate!' The impassioned words were like little blows raining on her face in the seconds before he bent his head and she was lost under the firm moving silkiness of his mouth. 'I fell in love with you,' he told her, when at last he could speak, 'the first time I saw

you, coming on to the ward with a vase of chrysanthemums the exact shade of your hair.'

'You can't have. You barked at me!'

'Self-defence,' he said, and kissed her again, unbut-
toning her coat, cupping her breasts, his hands moving
down her front, a groan breaking in his throat as she
arched towards him, her leg jamming his. 'Not
here…not now!' His voice was rough in her ear, he
was pulling the edges of her coat together, fastening
her seat belt and his, then starting the car, bumping it
off the grass verge.

'Where are we going?' Kate asked when she could
manage to speak.

'Home, of course.'

'Your home?'

'We've passed Ruston,' he said. 'I'm taking you
home to Cruse Cottage, then if you feel…' he allowed
a speeding van to pass them… 'the same about me
tomorrow, I'll call for you at midday, meet your mother
again and drive you to Ruston for lunch.'

'You think,' Kate said thickly, 'that I'm half-drunk,
don't you? You think…thought…that when I told you
I loved you, it was the champagne doing its work?
Well, it wasn't, although I agree, yes, it played a part.
What it did was give me the guts and courage to go
for gold!'

She heard him catch his breath. 'Don't, darling,
please, don't, or I'll be stopping the car again, and I
mustn't. I'm taking you home!'

'Well, so long as you believe me,' she said.

But he didn't, he couldn't, not absolutely, not until
the following day, not until the following afternoon
when, lying naked together under the big puffy duvet

in the master bedroom at Ruston House, they made love to one another, over and over again.

It was three-thirty and dusk was falling. Outside in the long garden the trees and shrubs were turning into pen-and-ink drawings, whilst a late-to-roost thrush, with supper in mind, cracked open a snail shell down on the stone-flagged path.

It was in the lull-time of loving when coherent thought was possible once more that Lucas asked Kate if she'd move in with him. 'Will you, Kate…will you?' Anxiety cracked his voice, and there was a tense taut-ness about his long body as he waited for her answer, which she was too surprised, too shocked to give—at least at first. But then she smiled—smiled and smiled—pulling his head down to hers.

'Yes, Lucas…my darling Lucas. Yes, I will,' she cried.

They made love again, this time more slowly, smooth as silk on silk, and afterwards, hungry for food, they went downstairs to eat the cold lunch Lucas had laid out for them four hours before—a lunch which, somehow or other, by some strange oversight, they'd completely forgotten about.

For the next six weeks, whilst the house purchase ar-rangements were going through, and whilst Kate was completing her rental time at Lew's, it was a case—when they wanted to be together—of, 'Your place or mine?' That always made them laugh. They moved into Ruston, which they furnished together, at the be-ginning of February, and in April, by absolutely mutual consent, they got married at the register office in Cletford, much to Paula's delight and to Gervase's mutterings of, 'Thank heavens, they've finally seen sense!' A crowd from the hospital came, including Chloe who, as big as a house, declared she would probably go into labour before she got home. Jean was there, with no sign of a limp. She had applied for Chloe's job and was on the shortlist of six. Kate hoped she'd get it. She herself had been lucky, so she felt, to get a full-time post at the hospital in Cletford, which meant, Lucas said, 'While at the beginning of each day we set off in opposite directions, at the end of every day we can come together, and once in our home we are one.'

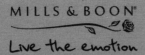

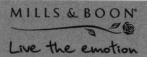

FREE!

4 Books
and a surprise gift!

We would like to take this opportunity to thank you for reading this Mills & Boon® book by offering you the chance to take FOUR more specially selected titles from the Medical Romance™ series absolutely FREE! We're also making this offer to introduce you to the benefits of the Reader Service™—

- ★ FREE home delivery
- ★ FREE gifts and competitions
- ★ FREE monthly Newsletter
- ★ Books available before they're in the shops
- ★ Exclusive Reader Service discount

Accepting these FREE books and gift places you under no obligation to buy; you may cancel at any time, even after receiving your free shipment. Simply complete your details below and return the entire page to the address below. *You don't even need a stamp!*

YES! Please send me 4 free Medical Romance books and a surprise gift. I understand that unless you hear from me, I will receive 6 superb new titles every month for just £2.60 each, postage and packing free. I am under no obligation to purchase any books and may cancel my subscription at any time. The free books and gift will be mine to keep in any case.

M4ZEE

Ms/Mrs/Miss/Mr ....Initials...............................
                                                                                BLOCK CAPITALS PLEASE

Surname..

Address..

....

....Postcode ....

Send this whole page to:
UK: The Reader Service, FREEPOST CN81, Croydon, CR9 3WZ
EIRE: The Reader Service, PO Box 4546, Kilcock, County Kildare (stamp required)